EVE'S ISLAND

EDGAR WALLACE

IAN HENRY PUBLICATIONS

Originally published by Gale & Polden, Ltd., 1909

This edition 1985

ISBN 0 86025 264 7

113053

Reprinted by Photobooks (Bristol) Ltd.
for Ian Henry Publications, Ltd.,
38 Parkstone Avenue, Hornchurch, Essex RM11 3LW

EDWARD G. TATHAM was born in Virginia in the United States of America. All the world knows that now. There are people in Springville, Va., who say they remember him as a child sitting before old Crubbs's Store twiddling his bare toes in the dust. A tow-headed boy they described him, with a long, serious face, and blue eyes that looked you through and through, as though you were a new variety of insect, or a fabulous freak of nature. They say too that he was talkative even in that far-away time, would recite conventional pieces, had a marvellous head for detail and was admitted to the debating society which forgathered daily at Crubbs's, on terms of equality.

This Mr. Crubbs the Elder told me himself, but I have advised my Government to attach little credence to his statement, because, I am informed, Crubbs is an inveterate remembrancer, and for a consideration would give you personal reminiscences of Abraham Lincoln, or for the matter of that, of George Washington.

Such meagre records as Springville affords point to the fact that Edward Garfield Tatham was born on April 1st, 1873, his father being Clark Thomas Tatham, his mother before marriage a Miss Georgina Mary Daly. They came from an Eastern State, Tatham senior being a dealer in horses, and they remained long enough in Springville to distinguish the town by producing the child who was afterwards to be a European *casus belli* (nearly), and then returned East.

The father died in Baltimore in '81, the mother in Troy, N.Y., in '84, and Edward G. Tatham, so far as I can ascertain, was reared by a Michael Joseph Daly who ran a pool room on the East Side. Daly became an Alderman, and was presumably a good man, for he died at a comparatively early age, and what happened to his nephew (for this was the relationship in which Edward Tatham stood) is rather a matter of conjecture than definite history.

At the age of twelve he crossed the Atlantic and took up his residency with some disreputable relations, to whose tender care Uncle Mike on his death-bed had consigned him, and he lived in a street very near to the Rotunda, Dublin.

I find that he was convicted and fined two shillings and sixpence for selling newspapers in the street. That is not an offence ; but the charge was " that he did on the 8th of October wilfully obstruct the Queen's highway, to wit Sackville Street, and when warned by Constable Patrick O'Leary, used insulting and abusive language calculated to cause a breach of Her Majesty's peace. Further, that he did assault and do injury to one Patrick Moriaty, an itinerant vendor of newspapers, aged 14, by striking him in the face."

I have seen in a newspaper file of the period an account of the trouble which rose as a result of young Tatham's first interference with vested interests—for Patrick Moriaty claimed the monopoly of selling *Freeman's Journals* in that particular section and resented the appearance of a newcomer.

Selling newspapers in Dublin was not young Tatham's *forte* ; three months later he was in London. He had severed his connection with his relatives—possibly, indeed probably, they had taken the initiative.

Of his life in London as a boy little is known. He worked, that is certain. But he was never more than two or three months in any one job. I have traced him to printers, shoemakers, and milk vendors. He seemed to be consumed with a spirit of restlessness which made the monotony of any form of employment maddening. " He just threw up and tried another stunt," said one authentic witness. It is certain that he attended the evening classes which a beneficent county council instituted for the benefit of those victims of neglected opportunity which abound. Here, for a few coppers payable weekly, he was perfected in the elements of education. He won a prize for practical chemistry worth much more than his year's school fees. One of his history essays was reprinted in the council magazine. He was quick to learn, immensely alert, " and," said a master who remembered him, " gifted with an extraordinary imagination." He had other qualities which were to come to fruition later.

I can picture him, a raw lank boy, crouched over the pine desk of the board school, hungry, for his salary, so far as I could learn, was never higher than $2.50 at the period, and more than half of that went in lodging.

" He was more hungry for knowledge," said the master ; " he devoured information as bears devour buns. As fast as one threw him a scrap he gobbled it. And if his food came too slowly, he reached out a paw the claws of which were notes of interrogation."

In '89 Tatham vanished. I can find no trail, no single clue of his movements. My own view is that he joined the British Army, but I have no support for this theory. Tatham himself is silent, and since I do not regard that period as being of vital importance in the compilation of the history, I have not pursued inquiries with any great diligence.

It was after the events which led to the assembling of our fleet in the Southern Atlantic, and when the name of Edward G. Tatham was on the lips of every man, woman, and child in the civilised world, that I was summoned to Washington to interview the President. He had previously been pleased to congratulate me on my history of the Spanish-American War—a history which I might claim in all modesty was as unprejudiced an account of actual happenings as was possible to collect so soon after the event.

I was ushered into his private office, and he shook hands with me warmly.

" It is good of you to come," he said with that expansive smile of his ; " I wanted to see you for reasons which are half official, half sentimental."

He paced up and down the apartment, his hands deep in his trousers' pockets.

" You know what has happened in the South Atlantic," he said. " You are aware that there has been a bother over President Tatham—trouble which is now happily at an end—and you know some of the causes which led up to that trouble ? "

I nodded. The story was common property.

" The English Government has held a secret commission," continued the President ; " it has been sitting for three weeks to root out the whys and the wherefores, and the evidence will never be published."

I nodded again.

" There is very little to learn," I said ; " we know that Tatham——"

He lifted his hand to stop me, and smiled.

" You know nothing," he said. " Do you know Eve Smith ? Do you know Callus the Correspondent ? Do you know Hackitt the engineer ? " he tapped the table before him and spoke deliberately. " Do you know the Scout ? "

I was puzzled.

" The Scout, Mr. President ? "

" It is a racehorse," he said, enjoying my bewilderment, " and the racehorse was the crux of the whole crisis—though few knew it, or know it now."

He opened a drawer in his desk, and took out a large envelope : from this he withdrew a number of sheets of paper.

" Here are the bones of the story," he said. " I have them through—er—diplomatic channels. Now I want you to go to Europe and encase these bones with flesh. You will find a list of people who will give you information—the British Government will offer no objection, once they understand that you know who the witnesses are. Tatham was a citizen of this country—he would be still if he had not made laws of his own—he has been in conflict with Europe and has won out. Do you go and tell us how he did it—good-bye, and a pleasant voyage."

And that is how I came to write the strangest book that has ever been written. A book with material for a good novel, if somebody more gifted than I care to take it in hand. And the fragments of the story, now presented to the English and American public for the first time, were collected in strange places.

For when I arrived in England many of the principal actors of the drama had scattered. The man Stuckey I interviewed in Wormwood Scrubbs prison, the war correspondent I ran to earth in a little *café* in Cadiz in the south of Spain, Sir James Calliper I found in Scotland, and fortunately he had the necessary blue books with him to elucidate his end of the story. Captain Ford I crossed Siberia to meet—his ship was on the China station —and Hackitt I met last of all in Rio de Janeiro.

Each of these witnesses was necessary. Their independent stories made the complete history of the most extraordinary adventure that ever man embarked upon.

The Congo Government side of the story I have not given. It was obviously prejudiced. In Brussels they regard Tatham as a vulgar thief, though he made generous reparation.

In piecing the story together I give the statements of the witnesses, not in the order in which they were given, but in such sequence as carries the story without a break.

I

THE EVIDENCE OF THE FIRST WITNESS :
CAPTAIN WALTER FORD, R.N., C.M.G.

Captain Walter Ford, Royal Navy, Companion of the Order of St. Michael and St. George, commanding the first-class cruiser *Ontario*. Captain Ford is a tall, spare man of fifty, slightly grey. He received me on board his ship off Hong Kong, and was a little stiff and reluctant to give me the information I required. Fortunately the letter which our Ambassador in London procured for me from the British Admiralty was sufficient to relieve him of every anxiety regarding a possible breach of the Official Secrets Act, and he told me all he had to tell concisely and briefly, with an admirable regard for essential facts.

" I was for some years in command of the survey ship *Charter*," said Captain Ford, " and I am well acquainted with the island which is now known as Tatham Island. As far as I can remember its exact position is Lat. 20.5.5 West, and Long. 37.15.4 South. I last visited the place in October, 1897, to take soundings at the northern side of the island. The island has all the appearance from the sea of being uninhabited, in fact it seems to be little more than a huge barren rock that rises perpendicularly from the water. It reminded me in conformation of an enormous iceberg. So unpromising was the aspect that it was only after considerable persuasion that I yielded, with great reluctance, to the suggestion of my chief officer that an attempt should be made to explore the interior.

" The island itself is ten miles in length, and at its widest point eight miles across.

" What finally decided me to make a more complete and searching examination was the discovery by the navigating officer, Lieutenant A. S. W. Sanders, R.N. This was no less than evidence of a subterranean river which apparently emptied itself on the south side of the island immediately beneath the cliff, which we named Signal Hill. The presence of fresh water had been unsuspected by those explorers who had from time to time sighted the island, and it was due to this fact that the sovereign claims of Great Britain had never been pushed home.

" Up to within two years ago the exact nationality of this island had not been determined, and its proprietorship was nebulous. It was claimed by Great Britain in conformity with the Tsai-Lang Treaty, by Portugal, as the result of an ' Occupation,' and by Holland. It is marked on all German maps as a German possession.

" On the discovery of the subterranean river I decided to make an investigation into the interior of the island, and in consequence, on the 28th of October, 1897, I despatched Lieutenant Granger, R.N., in the steam pinnace, with instructions to circumnavigate the island, and report upon possible landing-places.

" On his return he informed me that, notwithstanding a most painstaking search, he had failed to discover a foothold on the precipitous cliffs that formed the coastline. At only one spot had he been able to secure a landing, and that was on the northeastern side, where a strip of beach, totally covered at high water, but measuring 50 feet by 17 feet (from water's edge to the base of the cliff) at low water, enabled him to land.

" But from this spot, as from all others, so far as he could see, the rock rose to the height of 500 feet without a break or cranny that could afford foothold. So unusual were these features that, after perusing Lieutenant Granger's report, I myself made a personal inspection of the island, but with no better fortune than my officer. I should have returned without pursuing what appeared to be a fruitless search, but for the suggestion of Mr. Granger that a photograph might be taken of the interior of the island by means of a kite.

" A kite was accordingly rigged up, and the necessary apparatus to secure a picture was ingeniously improvised by Surgeon Doyle. Our first efforts were crowned with success : the camera worked satisfactorily. Before the plate was developed I sent the kite up again, but it was unfortunately carried away by a gust of wind.

" The third and fourth attempts were successful, and the photographs we secured were highly satisfactory. So far as we could see, the interior of the island was a great green valley, plentifully wooded and watered, with a number of small rivers converging towards the southern ' wall ' of the island. There was no sign of human habitation, but on enlarging the photograph there was evidence of abundance of game and of animal life—so far as I could make out : herds of animals resembling the South African quagga.

" Isochromatic plates were employed, which enabled me to gauge the geological formation ; especially do I refer to the range of hills that lines the inside of the western wall. Of these I reported :

" ' Have the appearance of being highly mineralized.'

" I concluded my soundings in December, at about which period I forwarded my report to the Lord of the Admiralty.

" I had at that time no idea of the existence of Captain Tatham. The island was known as the Ile de Desolation, or Woortz Island. I first heard of Captain Tatham when the rest of the world heard of him—in quite a casual way.

" My reports to the Admiralty were in the nature of confidential documents. I cannot say whether Captain Tatham had an opportunity of seeing them."

II

THE EVIDENCE OF THE SECOND WITNESS :
ERNEST GEORGE STUCKEY

The privilege of interviewing Ernest George Stuckey was granted by the Secretary of Home Affairs. The interview took place in the large prison in a suburb of London known as Wormwood Scrubbs. Here in the presence of two warders Stuckey told me his end of the story. A tall good-looking man, of smart appearance despite the hideous khaki of his prison clothes, the man looked what he was—an ex-soldier. He sat at the end of a ten-foot deal table and I at the other. The warders sat midway between us, one at each side of the table.

" I WAS at one time messenger at the Admiralty, but I am now undergoing sentence of twelve months' hard labour for a crime under the Official Secrets Act. Prior to my entering the service of the Admiralty," said Stuckey, " I was a corporal in the Artillery. I know the record room in the old Admiralty buildings, and was for some time in charge. There were many documents filed for reference to which I had access. They were confidential documents, but ' confidential ' is only a phrase, so far as certain army and navy documents are concerned, and is frequently added to a form or letter merely in accordance with regulations, when the contents are of no especial value either to the sender or the recipient.

" I have often amused myself by looking through some of the dockets, but I have seldom found anything worth the search. I might explain to you that my only object was to gratify an idle curiosity and to fill in the time.

" I remember reading Captain Ford's report on Tatham Island. It was numbered Ch. 7743, 1897. I believe the ' Ch ' stands for ' Charter,' the name of the ship commanded by the Captain. This report interested me very much, as I am naturally of an imaginative and romantic disposition, and I have spent many hours ' making up ' impossible stories about the island, and dreamt all kinds of wonderful dreams regarding its possibilities. I knew, and know Captain Ford's report by heart, and I could draw a plan of the island almost blindfolded. It was in 1899 that I first saw the chart, and became interested in it. Towards the end of that year the South African War broke out, and I was mobilized with the reserve and proceeded to South Africa on board the *Drayton Grange*.

" We were attached to General French for the greater part of the campaign, but towards the end, when the condition in the Cape Colony became serious, I was sent down with half a battery, under Captain Powell, of the Royal Horse Artillery, to join Henniker's column.

" It was very hard work, for Henniker kept us going day and night. He had half a regiment of a newly raised corps of irregulars with us, Kitchener's Fighting Scouts, as tough a lot as you could imagine, but tip-top fighters. That is where I first saw Captain Tatham.

" He was a tall man with a ready laugh, and eyes that looked you through and through, yet with a curious amused look, as if you were a new kind of caterpillar. He was a rare man when it came to fighting. He never seemed to know what fear was.

" I think he had been one of the original Rhodesian pioneers. I liked the look of him the moment I saw him, and, although he was an officer and I was one of the rank and file, we got quite chummy after a bit.

" This may sound strange, but it must be remembered that on active service, discipline, or what I might call ceremonial discipline, becomes relaxed ; and then again, an officer of an irregular force is not so strict in his relations with men as is an officer of the standing army.

" In the course of a chat with him one night I mentioned the Ford report, and he was very much interested. He got me to tell him half a dozen times over, and then I drew the map for him and gave him some rough idea as to the pictures that were taken by the kite.

" The ' highly mineralized ' paragraph in the report excited him most, and the next night he wrote down as much as I could remember of Captain Ford's statement in his field pocket-book.

" I thought he was American by his accent, and I was pretty sure I was right when he told me that he was a ' cosmopolitan,' because that is the name the Americans give themselves when they know little of their own country.

" He told me he had done a lot of prospecting, and could ' smell gold.' As far as I remember he commanded No. 2 Squadron of the Scouts, and his men were devoted to him. They were all his own men, men he had trekked with, and prospected with, and gone hunting with, and he used to call them by their Christian names, and more often than not they called him ' Ned.'

" What struck me about him was his extraordinary power of concentration. I've seen him sitting by his fire for hours on end, staring into the flame, with a look on his face such as I have seen on those of Buddhist priests in Burma.

" When he had finished thinking you could see he had whatever plan his mind was working at all cut and dried, and with no single detail unprovided for, and, whether it was a farm raid, or a bit of scouting, or a pitched battle, he had reviewed every possible combination of circumstances and provided for every contingency.

" This is how he struck me. I was brigaded with him until about six months before the end of the war, when he was sent with his regiment into the Pietersburg district, which is north of Pretoria, and I did not see him again until after the war.

" I heard rumours through some of his men whom I met at Wynberg Hospital—I was wounded in a fight with De Wet—that he was quarrelling with the Government over looted cattle.

" It appeared that there was a dispute as to his share of the prize money. I guess it was not his personal share that affected him, as much as the thought that his men were being unjustly treated. The upshot of it was that the Government behaved rather badly, and he came out of the business much poorer than when he went in.

" It was in June, 1902, that I met him again. I had taken my discharge, and was back again at the Admiralty, when I received a note from him asking me to meet him at Fregiloni's Restaurant off the Strand.

" He was still his old careless self, but looked curiously unnatural in his civilian clothing. He is the sort of man you cannot imagine out of riding-boots and slouch hat. I noticed that he appeared to be very poor. His boots were patched ; the edge of his collar was frayed, and his suit was obviously a ready-made one. We had a modest dinner, for which he paid, tipping the waiter handsomely. He told me he was in London with one of his men trying to raise money for an ' expedition.'

" The remainder of his squadron was at Cape Town waiting to hear from him. I asked how much money he wanted, and he said carelessly, ' About fifty thousand dollars '—which is one thousand pounds.

" Apparently he did not know a soul in London, and so far he had found no capitalist willing to advance him the money, or indeed any money at all.

" He also informed me that he had been offered a curious kind of a job by a Spanish-American firm in the City. He did not specify what it was, or what was its particular character. He had gone to the firm in the hope of raising the money, and they had apparently offered him an alternative adventure.

" I gathered this much from the scraps of talk he let fall. Apparently he had entertained the idea and had almost accepted, for he had gone into the matter very deeply, and there was a scene when he backed out, and a most solemn exchange of promises of secrecy. It sounded very mysterious, and at one time I thought Captain Tatham was romancing.

" He said he was returning to the Cape in a week, but there were one or two things to be done. I told him that I had a little money saved, some £20 in all, and that I was willing to lend him that, and, to my consternation, he accepted my offer readily. ' Every little helps now,' he said. The next day I sent the money to an address he gave me, and he sent back a receipt and a promissory note for £20.

" I did not see him again. Two days later I saw a paragraph in the evening papers that was headed ' A Remarkable Theft.' It was to the effect that some carmen engaged by Thomas Stence and Company, the balloon makers, had been instructed to deliver a small balloon at Hurlingham to the order of Count Castini, the famous aeronaut.

"Whilst the carman was taking his tea at a coffee shop in Brentford High Street, two men extracted the bale in which the little balloon was packed and made off with it.

"As one of the men wore the leather apron of a carter, the bystanders did not suspect anything, and the two thieves were allowed to go unchallenged. A full description of the men was published, and I had no difficulty in recognizing in the 'carman with the leather apron,' Captain Tatham.

"A week later he sailed, and I got a note from him, posted at Southampton, in which he remarked that 'despite almost over-whelming difficulties, we are slowly acquiring the equipment necessary to the successful issue of our expedition.' I was a little bewildered at the time, but very soon I began to realize the significance of his theft. I did not see Captain Tatham again. I have never seen him since.

"On October 28, 1906, a few days after the sensational victory of 'The Scout' in the Cesarewitch, I received by District Messenger a parcel despatched from the Chancery Lane Branch. Opening it, I discovered yet another parcel done up in wax paper. On the outside was fastened a label which read, 'It shall be returned to ye a hundred-fold—Ned Tatham.'

"Unwrapping the inner parcel I found a hundred banknotes each for £20. They were done up in bundles of fifty, and there were two such bundles. In December, of last year, in consequence of what transpired at Tatham Island, there was a departmental inquiry, as a result of which I was charged under Section 3 (c) of the Official Secrets Act—

"'Being entrusted in confidence with any document or information relating to . . . the military or naval affairs of His Majesty, and wilfully and in breach of such confidence communicating the same, when in the interest of the State it ought not to be communicated.'

"I was tried at the New Bailey, and sentenced to twelve months' imprisonment with hard labour.

"I have not since received any communication from President Tatham, nor have I ever heard of Mr. Hackitt or of the girl Eve Smith.

"The money he sent me is at my bank, the Court having decided that the payment was in relation to my loan to Tatham, and not to be regarded as remuneration for information received."

III

THE EVIDENCE OF THE THIRD WITNESS: WILLIAM C. HACKITT

William C. Hackitt was a sturdy, thick-set man of fifty. He was prosperous-looking, and apparently he has quite a bunch of money invested in real estate in Rio—where I met him.

He was an interesting type of American seaman—better educated than most men who have lived their lives afloat, cautious of speech and exact of statement. I have only given part of his story, the latter portion being identical with that told by the correspondent Callus—except that the latter's statement is considerably more detailed and probably, since he shared the confidence of Tatham, more accurate.

" I AM a native of Seattle, Washington, and by profession I am a seaman. I first went to sea in 1872 on the sailing vessel *Star of the West*, 'Frisco to Boston.

" I served before the mast for ten years before I got my mate's certificate in an English ship. I earned a master's ticket in 1889, and three years later I entered the service of the Coastwise line, being appointed second officer on the steamship *O'sango* trading between Liverpool and Cabinda.

" In '95 the company extended its operations, shipping freights to the Cape and Natal in competition with the Castle and Bucknall Lines. I was promoted to be chief officer of *O'laki* in 1901 at a salary of $40 a month. The work was hard, we were under-officered, and, to make matters worse, I very soon discovered that the captain of the *O'laki* drank heavily.

" We started our homeward voyage for Durban, Natal, in January, 1902.

" One day out, the second officer went sick, which meant that the navigation and the care of the ship devolved upon myself and the third officer. We were due to call at Port Elizabeth, and we entered the Bay in a strong north-easterly gale.

" It was rather dubious as to the advisability of anchoring, especially as the gale showed signs of increasing in strength, and the glass continued to fall. I communicated my doubts to the skipper, who was in his cabin sleeping off the effects of a drinking bout.

" He gruffly ordered me to anchor. This I did, at what I considered to be a safe distance from the shore. The wind increased in velocity, and at half-past three the harbour master signalled, ' Get to sea with all despatch.'

" I reported this to the skipper, who, however, told me to ignore the signal. I was considerably scared, but I flew, ' Have decided to remain ' in answer to the shore signal. As a cautionary measure I ordered the third officer to stand by to let go the storm anchor. At five o'clock our cable parted, and I dropped over the drogue, but there was no checking our drift, and I hoisted ' N.C.'

" We went ashore at six p.m., and the crew was rescued by the Port Elizabeth lifeboat. The ship was a total wreck. At the Board of Trade inquiry my captain stated that the warning of the harbour master had not been conveyed to him, that he was in his berth ill at the time, and that I was in sole charge of the ship, and that the responsibility for obeying or disobeying the signal was mine.

" As a result of this lie, I was adjudged by the Board to have been guilty of unseamanlike conduct, and my certificate was suspended.

" The agents of the company paid me my salary, and informed me that they were advised by cable that the company had no further use for my services. Thus I found myself stranded in Port Elizabeth with some $200 and no prospects whatever.

" Luckily for me, the s.s. *Inkonka*, a Rennie boat, was in the Bay, commanded by Captain Moore, a big-hearted seaman of the old type, who offered me an opportunity of working my passage home as bo'sun. This, however, I declined. I was sick of seafaring and wanted a rest.

" I fixed up a passage on board the ship, and sailed for Cape Town a week after the finding of the Court. The *Inkonka*, although nominally a cargo boat, has excellent accommodation for passengers, and I found myself in clover, for the food was most excellent and the officers were a decent lot of men.

" There were no other passengers but myself, and, so far as the Captain knew, there was little likelihood of anybody coming aboard at Cape Town. But, to our surprise, on reaching that port we were informed by the agents that a party of fifty had booked passages for Loanda—that is, St. Paul de Loanda—which was our next port of call.

" Captain Moore was a little mystified by this unusual passenger list and pointed out the difficulty of accommodating so large a party, but the agent stated that the party were prepared to rough it, and their rates had been adjusted on that assumption. He furthermore explained that it consisted of a party of prospectors who were going to tramp through Portuguese territory to the Katanga in search of minerals.

" The party came aboard that afternoon. A harder crowd of citizens I have never struck ; they were all men who had apparently seen service during the recent war, and each was armed with a Mauser rifle and a bandolier of ammunition, which I was informed represented Boer loot.

" In addition, their equipment consisted of picks, shovels, and the rough cradles that I have seen miners use in the Australian alluvial fields. Yet for all their tough appearance, they were a quiet, orderly lot of men, and there did not seem to be an ounce of whisky between the party. The leader was a singularly striking man, who was variously addressed as 'Captain Tatham' and 'Ned,' and his authority appeared to be absolute.

"I found Captain Tatham a most charming companion. Apparently he had a nodding acquaintance with every country in the world, and he even had a fair working knowledge of sea-manship, having as a boy shipped before the mast.[1]

"Very naturally, with my grievance uppermost in my mind, I confided to him the story of the wreck of the *O'laki*, and not only was he sympathetic, but he seemed unusually interested. He inquired as to whether I was a married man, what were my prospects, what I intended to do for a living on my return to America, and I told him I was single, and that my prospects were nil, and that for all I knew I should starve, or else go to sea again before the mast.

"He asked me in all seriousness whether I should like to be a pirate, and I answered jokingly that such a life had its attraction.

"We reached Lobito Bay after a pleasant voyage of six days, and, landing some railway material, continued our journey up the coast. It was the night before we reached Loanda that Captain Tatham made his proposition to me. It was the offer of the mastership of the *Pealo*.

"I had frequently seen the *Pealo*. She was a steamer of 900 tons, and was employed by the Government of the Congo Free State to carry mails and telegrams between Loanda and Broma.

"You must understand that the Congo Free State had no direct cable communication with the outer world, and cables were either sent via Brazzaville over a thousand miles of land wire to a port in French West Africa, or by boat to Loanda for transmission.

"The latter method was more usually adopted.

"For this purpose the *Pealo* was employed. She was a little craft with a remarkable history. She had been wrecked on the rocks that abound near Matadi, and had remained high and dry for twelve months before a wandering engineer had salved her, first purchasing the wreck for something like $250. By blasting away the rocks that pierced her hull, and making her roughly watertight with cement, he got her beached and put into working order.

"I told Captain Tatham that I knew the history of the ship, but I could not understand his offer, unless, indeed, he held some high office under the Congo Government and was in a position to

[1] This possibly explains the disappearance of Tatham from London and the difficulty of tracing his history as a youth.

confer the mastership. He seemed very much amused at my answer, and replied—

" ' You must understand, Mr. Hackitt, that I am in a very difficult position, and although I am not able to confide my plans to you, yet I may elucidate the situation by setting forth the following primal and vital facts.

" ' (1) I am engaged in carrying through an expedition which, were it properly equipped and every contingency provided for, would cost some £15,000.

" ' (2) So far my outlay has been £75 16s. 4d. This has covered all preliminary expenses other than the expedition fare, which the expedition has paid for itself. I have computed the further expenditure necessary, as follows :—

Purchase of steamship for purpose of expedition	$35,000
Victualling and coaling same	9,000
Wages	4,250
Scientific equipment	14,000
Provisions and field equipment	1,000
Sundries	6,750
Making a total of	$70,000

" ' (3) Face to face with these liabilities, I have the knowledge that the combined capital of the expedition is about fifty dollars net.'

" I asked him under these circumstance how he reconciled his offer of the mastership of the *Pealo*. I pointed out that under any circumstances the *Pealo* being a government ship would not be for sale. His reply was simple.

" ' We must borrow the *Pealo*,' he said quite seriously ; ' in other words, we must steal her.'

" He extracted no promise of secrecy from me before he made this remarkable statement, but as I was afterwards to learn, he was a very keen judge of character, and I have no doubt he had sized me up pretty well.

" ' It is regrettable that such a course is necessary, but unfortunately the old adventurous spirit, that in the days of Elizabeth led the London merchant to finance the privateering craft of the Spanish Main, is utterly and totally dead, and it is necessary for the success of the expedition that we should possess a steamer. I have chosen the *Pealo*, because it belongs to an unpopular Government, in fact a Government that isn't a Government at all. No court of law with a sense of humour would pursue a charge of piracy brought by the Congo Free

State—the very idea is so grotesquely comic that the case would laugh itself out of court. Now, as to you,' he said, addressing me, ' you are a broken man. You have nothing to lose and everything to gain, and if things go wrong I give you my word of honour that I will establish your innocence.'

" He then went on to give me elaborate particulars regarding the object of the expedition. I cannot truthfully say that I thought overlong on the offer Captain Tatham made to me. Indeed I believe I accepted it on the spot.

" The next day we reached Loanda and Captain Tatham landed. The *Pealo* was lying at her moorings, having arrived the night previous. I observed her with greater interest. She was a neat, compact-looking little craft, bearing the stamp of seaworthiness that any sailor could distinguish a mile away.

" She was flying the flag of the Congo State, which is a five-pointed golden star on a royal blue background. Although Tatham went ashore none of his men accompanied him. He told me he intended arranging the direct transfer of the men from one ship to the other, owing to the stringent Portuguese regulations which forbid the importation of firearms.

" The *Inkonka* was due to leave at eight, but it was not until seven o'clock that Captain Tatham returned. He said he had fixed up the passages by representing his party as being Italian labourers for the new Stanley Falls railway. He said he had arranged to pay the fares when the men were on board. He also told me that he had ordered enormous stores of provisions to be sent off to the *Pealo*, and had practically cleared out the floating stock of the Loanda stores.

" These also he had arranged to pay for on delivery. Somehow this scheme was less palatable to me than the larger and more serious matter of the ship, and I ventured to express my opinion to Captain Tatham.

" He listened to me with great patience, and indeed I have never known him to display the least unwillingness to accept and analyse criticism.

" ' You have lost sight of one fact,' he said, when I had finished. ' What I am doing is not stealing, it is simply coercing credit. Every penny's worth of stores I take from Loanda I shall pay for sooner or later. I shall even recompense King Leopold's Government for the inconvenience it may suffer from the temporary detachment of his fleet.'

" I am a self-educated man and am not prepared to point out the flaws in Captain Tatham's code of morality, but at the time I was perfectly satisfied that such a flaw existed and just as satisfied to accept his explanation.

" We boarded the *Pealo* at six bells in the third watch, rowing off from the *Inkonka* in two of that ship's boats. I said ' Goodbye ' to Captain Moore, who saw nothing remarkable in my change of plans. He must have realised that I was a ruined man so far as the sea was concerned, and did not blame me for joining the ' prospecting party.'

" We were received at the gangway of the *Pealo* by the second officer. There was only a dim gangway light, so that the arms of the party, which were concealed as far as possible, passed without observation. We found our stores piled up on the deck, with two or three European clerks waiting to complete the sale. There were cases of milk, cases of preserved beef, biscuits, sacks of potatoes, bags of rice, flour, and grain. Sugar and salt, tea by the dozen chests, and coffee by the hundredweight.

" Tatham had a brief interview with the clerks. I gathered rather than heard that he requested them to call the following morning, and with some demur they consented. I heard him pointing out that the *Pealo* was not due to leave until the following afternoon, and heard him refer to ' money ' and ' cable.' When they had rowed away the following conversation took place between the second officer of the *Pealo*—a M. Jacobus van Held and Captain Tatham :—

" *Van Held :* ' We will now arrange the matter of the fares for your party, Monsieur Tatham.'

" *Tatham :* ' Will that not do in the morning ? '

" *Van Held :* ' I would rather the matter were settled to-night. From Loanda to Boma the fare is 100 francs.'

" *Tatham :* ' That will be 5100 francs—is there no reduction for a large party ? '

" *Van Held :* ' Absolutely none.'

" *Tatham :* ' I would like to see the Captain.'

" *Van Held :* ' He is ashore. I am the only officer on board.'

" *Tatham :* ' I think I know the chief engineer—may I have a word with him ? '

" *Van Held :* ' He is also ashore ; with the exception of myself and a mechanician on duty and a steward, there is nobody on board.'

" *Tatham :* ' Why have you the mechanician ? ' (*i.e.* engine-room artificer).

" *Van Held :* ' Because we must keep steam on—that is the regulation. But I would rather discuss the question of fares.'

" Then ensued a long argument, partly in Flemish and partly in French, both of which languages I imperfectly understand, and the ' mechanician ' was summoned from below to support the officer. The end of it was, the second officer with the mechanician left the ship to summon the captain, with the hint of a threat that on their return they would be accompanied by the representatives of Portuguese law.

"From the point of view of an American seaman, to leave a ship with no competent person in charge was just mad, but they do queer things on Belgian ships. As their boat pushed off, I saw three of Tatham's men go nipping down the steel ladder that led to the engine-room, and in about a minute one of them shouted, 'All right.'

"I was surprised to see another go forward to the bow with the agility of a born seaman. Tatham and I walked forward to the bridge. 'You are in charge,' said Tatham.

"So I rung the engine 'Slow ahead,' to ease the mooring cable. I heard the pin knocked out and the cable fall with a splash in the sea, and felt the vessel riding free. Tatham turned and ordered all lights out, and I sent the telegraph over to 'half ahead' setting the course west and a point north. 'Stand right out to sea,' said Tatham at my elbow. 'I will give you the course to-morrow.'"

IV

THE EVIDENCE OF THE THIRD WITNESS : WILLIAM C. HACKITT
(*continued*)

Hackitt's statement was conveyed in two interviews. He spoke according to the book in the sense that he had elaborate notes and a diary to which he referred. In the second interview, in his anxiety for accuracy, he made several corrections of the foregoing narrative, but none of any consequence. In the main they dealt with trifling discrepancies of dates.

The reader will observe that Mr. Hackitt employs excellent English, and I suspect the influence of Eve Smith in this matter, though the subject is too delicate for me to question Hackitt about.

"THE next morning Captain Tatham came to me with a half-smile as though something had amused him.

"'We have kidnapped a newspaper correspondent,' he said, and told me that in one of the steamer's cabins he had discovered, asleep and unconscious of the change that had come over the fortunes of the ship, a Mr. Callus, a correspondent who had been engaged investigating the condition of Angola and the charges of slave trading brought against the Government.

"A few minutes later Mr. Callus came on deck.

"He was a man of about thirty, of medium height. He wore his moustache brushed up in the German fashion. He tackled Tatham and demanded an explanation, which the Captain very readily gave him, to my surprise giving a frank account both of his plans and the happenings of the previous night.

"Callus listened in silence, but I could see that, being a reporter and on the look-out for a startling piece of news, he wasn't sorry to be with us.

"' You will of course understand, Captain Tatham,' he said, ' that I am not in this business of yours. I shall probably give evidence against you at your trial, and be present when you're hanged, but my interest is the interest of the observer. I shall write you a formal protest against being carried off against my will, and shall expect you to regard me as a prisoner of war.'

"I was surprised afterwards to learn that Mr. Callus was not Scotch, but Irish. Captain Tatham agreed, and the two went below to breakfast. I forgot in my evidence yesterday to say that the one article of hold baggage possessed by the expedition was a huge bale carefully packed and roped, which was handled with extraordinary care. I should imagine it weighed about three-quarters of a hundredweight. After breakfast Captain Tatham gave me the course. We were then about a hundred miles west of Loanda. I immediately changed the course to S.W. by W.

"I knew what is now called Tatham Island by repute. It lies about ten degrees to the north-west of Tristan da Cunha and is about 950 miles from Rio.

"Speaking generally, the voyage was a pleasant one. Three days out we had squally weather and a beam sea that kept the *Pealo* on the roll, but we only carried this weather for half a day. What surprised me about the voyage was the remarkable aptitude shown by the men for sea work, and I am inclined to believe that, of Captain Tatham's mixed company, a very fair percentage had at some time in their lives followed the sea as a profession.

"The seamanship of these men and their remarkable willingness (such of them as were new to the life) to learn, removed one of the anxieties that had been with me since this extraordinary voyage started.

"The other worry, however, was not so easily removed. Immediately after we left port I had made an examination of the bunkers, and found to my satisfaction that the ship had been coaled—probably on the day before our arrival. Mr. Callus confirmed this supposition. But, even so, it was apparent to me that there was not sufficient fuel for a 3000 miles voyage, and I mentioned this fact to Captain Tatham.

"By keeping our speed down to a minimum we might eke out our coal supply to last 2000 or even 2500 miles steaming, but even supposing we reached the island, we would be to all intents and purposes a derelict if we were without the necessary fuel to make the return trip. As in all other matters, Captain Tatham was remarkably optimistic.

" ' I have thought of that,' he said, ' and I've ordered a coal ship from Pernambuco to meet us.'

" I was somewhat staggered by this statement, but when he gave me the precise latitude and longitude (I think it was 10 West 16 South, as near as I can recollect) in which we were to pick up the collier, I realized that I had to do with a most resourceful man.

" The weather continued fine, Captain Tatham suggested that an excellent opportunity presented itself for changing the appearance of the ship, and to this I agreed. There was a fair quantity of paint in the ship's stores, and we found in the ship's hold a number of tins consigned to Matheson and Deal of Boma.

" So I got the men to work, a number slung over the ship's side being engaged in turning the hull of the *Pealo* from its smart whiteness to a dirty slate colour, very much like that adopted in the Royal Navy. The funnel was treated in the same way, and all the upper works were also ' painted out.' The name *Pealo* was indicated by gun-metal letters, and these we removed and dropped into the sea, and the word ' Scoutina ' substituted. I asked Captain Tatham how he arrived at the name, and he said it was feminine for ' Scout,' and was chosen to remind the crew of their connection with Kitchener's Scouts during the war.

" When the painting had been completed, he started his men to work rigging up queer contrivances out of canvas and some spare derrick gear. I asked Mr. Callus, who smiled and said that Captain Tatham was working the naval manœuvre racket— that the *Scoutina* was going to play the ass in the lion's skin. I did not ask Tatham what the scheme was, knowing that in fulness of time he would tell me. Seven days out, and as nearly as possible 100 miles south-west of St. Helena, we sighted a steamer right ahead. I had been figuring things out, and when Tatham told me that this must be the *Canker*—our collier—I ventured to express my amazement that he could have arranged so far ahead—for Pernambuco was 21 days' sail from the rendezvous.

" He then told me that when he had been in London he had been offered a very lucrative appointment. He gave me no further information, and left me just as puzzled as ever, for I could see no connection between the appointment he had been offered in London and our picking up with the collier in mid-ocean. The only further thing he said was : When the *puljanes* came down on the *tao* they can afford to pay for their amusement. To-day they'll pay in coal.' This was all gibberish to me, and it was not till very recently, when I read the ' History of the Philippines,' that I saw its significance. When we came within signalling distance, Captain Tatham told me to fly the Belgian ensign and the signal ' P. T. X. O.,' which I did, the ship answering ' L. B.'

" On consulting my signal-book I saw that these could not possibly be intelligently translated by the commercial code, and gathered from that that we were making prearranged signals. We slowed down till we lay at two cables' length from each other.

" The sea was perfectly smooth with a slight swell, but I did not consider it advisable to get any closer. The collier had a boat lowered and there came on board the master of the *Canker*— an elderly seaman to whom Captain Tatham introduced himself.

" After a brief interview, which seemed to pass off to the satisfaction of Captain Giles (the master of the *Canker*), the work of coaling ship began.

" Naturally it was a tedious and wearisome business, but Captain Tatham, with extraordinary ingenuity, got a hawser-carrier rigged between the two ships, by means of which the work was to some extent lightened, but night was near at hand before the last load was put on board.

" The captain of the collier had expressed his surprise at the smallness of our ship ; from the quantity of coal he had brought he had evidently expected a craft of 4000 or 5000 tons, but in a few smooth sentences Captain Tatham had settled any doubt that might have been in the skipper's mind.

" We had previously cleared out all the holds for the reception of the coal, and when the coaling operations had been completed, and Tatham and the skipper had had a parting drink, I made an inspection below and found that we had enough coal on board for eight weeks' continuous steaming.

" We signalled ' Good-bye ' and steamed away, the *Canker* going due north-west, and we were continuing west and a point south till she was out of sight.

" Then Captain Tatham instructed me to alter our course, and we doubled back eastward, then northward, then southward again, until the following morning found us as nearly as possible in the place where we had coaled the day previously.

" At daybreak the whole crew was engaged in cleaning away the signs of coaling, and in rigging up the canvas contrivances of which I spoke. Mr. Callus sat on the bridge with me smoking a cigar, and taking a keen interest in all that was happening. He had been locked in his cabin during the coaling operations, as a precautionary measure. Whilst the ' crew ' were fixing the canvas and booms under the direction of Captain Tatham, Callus kept up a running fire of caustic criticism, and it was from this that I began to realize that the plan was to alter the appearance of the *Scoutina* until she resembled a gun-boat.

" Wooden guns were mounted fore and aft, a tiny fighting top was constructed out of canvas on the foremast, and two small ventilators projecting over the edge had the appearance of quick firers.

" This touch seemed to annoy Callus.

" ' Who ever saw a gun-boat with fighting tops ! ' he exclaimed ; and Tatham grinned.

" ' It's a new idea,' was his reply.

" A whole day passed without incident, but at eight bells in the afternoon watch of the second day a steamer came over the horizon.

" She headed straight for us.

" We made no sign till she ran up the British flag, then at Tatham's order I flew the White Ensign.

" I did it with some qualms, because it is a serious matter to masquerade as a British man-o'-war, but Tatham seemed to regard his act without concern.

" The ship could not have been half a mile distant when we broke our ensign, but the effect was electrical, for she heeled over and swung round in a wide circle, as though she'd thought of a sudden engagement in the north and was anxious to keep it.

" We had all our flags ready. Tatham had spent the whole morning sorting them out and patching them up, and we signalled—

" ' Heave to, I am coming aboard.'

" She made no answer, and Tatham signalled—

" ' Heave to, or I'll sink you.'

" To that she answered—

" ' Cannot understand.'

" Nevertheless she slowed down, and Tatham asked—

" ' What ship is that ? '

" She answered—

" ' *Greenwich Hove.* London to Philippines. General cargo.'

" Tatham rearranged his flags, and said—

" ' I am coming on board to see your papers. Open up hold No. 3 for inspection.'

" It was one of the most mysterious messages I had ever seen sent, and was on a par with his extraordinary knowledge of the collier.

" The ship made no reply for a while, then she put up—

" ' Have infectious disease on board.'

" I heard Tatham guffaw as we decoded the message.

" ' Am sending a doctor—stop your engines or I'll disable you.

" With that she stopped, and we came up with her.

" It was now close on sunset, and by Tatham's order I steamed slowly to the westward of the steamer.

" I think his idea was to come between the light and the *Greenwich Hove*, so that the spurious character of our armaments should not be detected. We lay off about eight cables from the steamer, and one of our wooden guns was ostentatiously turned in her direction.

" A boat was lowered, and Tatham sprang into it with half a dozen men.

" There was a certain uniformity about their appearance— they wore blue jerseys and were hatless—that might very easily deceive the casual observer. They rowed beautifully too. I think, though, that I was the most naval-looking member of the party, because I was clean-shaven and wore my 'company' jacket, and the Coastwise Line had chosen the badges of rank worn by their officers to correspond with the Royal Navy badges.

" They lowered the gangway for us and Tatham went up, followed by myself.

" There was a group of officers standing at the head of the gangway, and they looked suspiciously at Tatham in his civilian dress, and in a most unfriendly way at me.

" Tatham introduced himself.

" ' I am the British Vice-Consul from Benguela, and I am deputed by the Consul at St. Paul de Loanda to make a search of your ship.'

" ' You have a warrant ? ' asked the commander.

" For answer Tatham waved his hand in the direction of the ' warship.'

" ' There is my warrant,' he said,

" ' For what are you searching ? ' the Captain demanded.

" ' Contraband of war,' said Tatham coolly. ' You are carrying arms to the Philippines for the use of the Puljanes ; you are carrying them at the order of Señor de Costa of the firm of De Costa Riez and Co., of Little Saville Street, E.C. You were instructed to pick up a collier here, and proceed on your voyage.'

" ' You seem to know all about it,' said the skipper ; ' there are fourteen cases consigned to the Philippines, they are described on my bills as " hardware." I know nothing more.'

" Tatham bowed.

" ' You will be good enough to get your boats out and bring these cases alongside the gun-boat,' he said. ' You may then continue your voyage, reporting the circumstances to the British Consul at your first port of call.'

" ' Suppose I refuse ? ' asked the Captain.

" Tatham looked very grave. He entered so thoroughly into the part he played that for the moment he *was* the British Consul.

" ' In that case,' he said, ' I shall have no other course open but to instruct Commander Smith ' (here he indicated me with a nod) ' to place you under close arrest, and to convey your ship into the nearest port.'

" The Captain hesitated, then turned to his second and gave orders for the boats to ' go away.'

" It was dark when the first consignment came alongside.

" We allowed nobody aboard, but got a derrick out and cranked the arms on board, package by package. As fast as they came Tatham had them opened. The consignment included 100 Winchester rifles and 20,000 rounds of ammunition, but what seemed to please Tatham most was a maxim gun with tripod and spare parts.

" We were hoisting in the last crate when the skipper's voice hailed us over the side.

" ' What do you want ? ' said Tatham.

" ' I want to come aboard,' said the skipper.

" Tatham thought a little, then he gave orders to throw over a monkey ladder, and the skipper came up hand over fist.

" All lights had been extinguished on the deck, the big branch lamp which we had used for taking in the arms being swung over the side at such an angle as to throw a light on the laden boats, without revealing the peculiarities of our deck hamper.

" But the old man was shrewd enough. There was some reflection of our light from the sea, and his quick glance at the ' guns ' and the dummy ' casemates ' told him all he wanted to know. He turned on Tatham, but I could see Tatham fingering his revolver.

" ' What is the meaning of this ? ' said the skipper.

" ' Piracy,' said Tatham, as coolly as you please, ' which is only one degree more respectable than carrying arms to half-breed cut-throats.'

" Those were his very words, and the old skipper seemed choked.

" When he got his voice, he said—

" ' You'll have to answer for this, my friend.'

" ' Not at all,' said Tatham, ' any more than you will ' ; and then he started to talk as I have often heard him. He had a trick of speech-making (he told me once he had run for the Membership of the Legislative Assembly in Rhodesia) and, like somebody else I've read about, had a way of talking to you as though you were a public meeting. I have a good memory for things of that kind, and although I may not be exact to a word or two it is impressed almost word for word on my mind. This is how he started—

" ' It is difficult to appreciate in how so far the doctrine falsely ascribed to the Jesuits, that evil may be done that good may result, is justified in practice. Here we have a problem which exemplifies the plausibility of such a theory. A is a firm engaged in nefarious traffic, B is a shipowner furthering the immoral objects of A, C is a person himself questionably employed, who in order to further schemes which on first inspection may appear to be of a dubious character, utilizes the guilt of A and the complicity of B. In doing so he commits an illegal act, which has the effect of preventing A from committing one many degrees worse——'

" ' I don't want a speech or a blooming sum in proportion,' interrupted the skipper roughly. ' I want your name, and the name of this ship.'

" Tatham said nothing. I have sometimes thought he was a singularly vain man, for he could easily be ruffled by any remark that reflected upon what he considered to be his especial personal gifts. And I have reason to know that he greatly prided himself upon two qualities, one of which was his power of delivery, and the other his attainments as a writer of despatches. He walked to the side of the ship where the ladder hung and pointed to it.

" ' That is your way, Captain. Let me advise you to go whilst you're safe.'

" The Captain obeyed : there was something in Tatham's voice that was very ominous. We saw the boats row back to the side of the *Greenwich Hove*, then, with all our lights out, we set a course due south.

" If I remember rightly, I have already told you that Captain Tatham confided his plans to Mr. Callus, the newspaper correspondent. Mr. Callus knew something of the island. He reminded us of the wreck of the *Queen of Plata* in 1872. It had been of particular interest to the English people at the time. In July of that year the Middle Park Stud had been sold, and a number of thoroughbreds purchased on behalf of the Argentine Stock Company had been despatched by the *Queen of Plata* to South America. The ship had been driven out of its course by severe gales, her propeller shaft had broken, and nothing was ever heard of her until a bottle was picked up in which was a brief message that she had gone down with all hands off the Ile de Desolation.

" ' It was before I was born, of course,' said Mr. Callus, in a tone which suggested that this was the weak point in the story, but although I myself was young at the time, I remembered the particulars very clearly.

" Tatham was interested and asked whether the ship had

carried specie, and at what point of the island she foundered, and whether salvage operations had ever been attempted. You may gather from that simple inquiry that Captain Tatham, although he was out for a big stake, by no means despised the smaller fish that might be drawn into his net.

" I remember the night of that talk very well. It was the night after we parted company from the *Greenwich Hove*, and we were sitting on the little navigation bridge. The moon was at its full, the sea calm as a mill pond, and no sound broke the silence save the ' throb, throb ' of the screw. It was the sort of night when your thoughts stray to the Homeland and to those who are near or dear, and whilst there were few in all America who cared whether I lived or died, yet there were some whose images came to my mind and filled me with an irritating sadness.

" Nothing seemed to depress Tatham, however ; he was as cheerful as a cricket, so cheerful that Callus set himself, out of sheer cussedness, to tone him down. We had been discussing the island, and Tatham had been talking largely of methods for conveying the gold to England. He would, he said, work the alluvial first, till a large enough quantity had been collected, then he would send the *Scoutina* to England to dispose of it and to buy machinery for working the reef.

" ' Supposing there is no alluvial,' said Callus.

" ' In that case,' said Tatham, ' we must work the quartz as best we can.'

" ' Suppose there is no quartz—no gold at all, in fact,' suggested Callus.

" Tatham clicked his lips impatiently, and began one of his public addresses.

" ' There is no more convincing and alarming evidence of incipient insanity,' he said, ' than that afforded by the inability to argue vital questions to a logical conclusion. In contradistinction to this, there is no viler use to which the human imagination may be put to than the anticipation of difficulties. All human effort is so much waste force, if behind the will to do, there lurks the fear of failure.'

" Mr. Callus yawned.

" ' Cut it out,' he said.

" Though Tatham dismissed the possibility of failure so easily I could see that the thought worried him. He had one of his day-dreams—I can think of no other description for them—and sat three hours on end with his feet cocked up on the rail staring into space.

" I happened to be by his side when he recovered and he

turned to me, just as though we were continuing the conversation of the night before last, and said—

"'Even if gold is absent, there is no reason why other minerals, or even diamonds, should not exist on the island.'

"Five days after this we sighted the island.

"Its first appearance is like that of Table Mountain, except that instead of sloping gradually left and right as Table Mountain appears to slope when seen from the sea, its walls fall sheer. The nearer we got to it the more wall-like its shore appeared. I approached cautiously, for, in spite of the soundings recorded on Captain Ford's chart, I was by no means certain that we might not discover the submerged reef upon which it is understood the *Queen of Plata* sank.

"I had men in the chains taking soundings and slowed down to quarter speed. We were unable to get bottom at twenty fathoms, and we gradually drew nearer the rock. I then got over a deep-sea lead—we had patent sounding apparatus in the chart-room, but I did not see the necessity for using it.

"I found bottom at sixty fathoms and anchored.

"The weather had continued fine, and the sea smooth to moderate, but in the lee of the island it was like a sheet of glass.

"It was too late to do anything that night, save to get Captain Tatham's baggage on deck—the bale of which I have spoken, and which when opened proved to be a small balloon.

"I was then to understand the reason for certain of Captain Tatham's 'purchases' at Loanda. One of these which puzzled me was a carboy of some acid, and a number of sacks of some weighty material which had been stowed away below.

"I have a very elementary knowledge of practical chemistry, but I know enough to realize now that the sacks contained zinc shavings, and that Captain Tatham intended to generate hydrogen for the inflation of the silk envelope.

"The process of filling the balloon occupied the greater part of the next day. Fortunately for us, there was little or no wind.

"The operation was, I think, rather hampered than helped by Captain Tatham himself, who in the very middle of it was seized with an idea. This was no other than that the buoyancy of the balloon might be increased by the admixture of some fancy gas that he had thought out, and which he instantly christened 'Tathomegen.'

"I do not know the formulæ of this new element, but I understand that it was produced by passing equal volumes of oxygen and hydrogen through steam. Half a day was wasted in the generation of the necessary oxygen, which unfortunately refused to answer the tests that Tatham and Callus applied, and the Captain was regretfully compelled to continue filling his balloon as he had commenced.

" We had an anxious time that night, however, for one of those sudden squalls for which these seas are famous sprang up and the balloon almost carried away. About one o'clock in the morning we had a consultation, and it was decided to deflate the balloon in spite of the fact that we had not sufficient chemicals to generate a further supply of gas. Tatham, however, was optimistic. He had a scheme for producing coal gas—he had thought of it in the night—and I am under the impression that he was seriously disappointed when the wind abated as suddenly as it had arisen, and the necessity for deflating passed.

" I have not yet described very fully the appearance of the island, but what struck me was its singular smoothness. That is, the polished appearance of the cliffs. It was as though somebody had gone over them with emery-paper and leather, and had polished them until they shone. On the north side of the island there was no break in the continuity of the ' wall,' on the eastern side there was an almost perpendicular flaw—a huge rent that split the rock from summit to base. There was no appearance of any possible foothold.

" The subterranean river we discovered without any difficulty, the roof of the tunnel through which the river poured was plainly visible at low water. At the time I thought Captain Ford had made an unnecessary mystery of the existence of this river, which was plainly discernible, but afterwards I had reason to change my opinion. The morning of our landing was bright and summery. We had anchored to the north of the island, and such wind as there was N.N.W., a point W. This was favourable to our plans, and at twelve o'clock Captain Tatham and one of his men (a man named Taunton) stepped into the sling which had been improvised and the rope by which it was attached paid out.

" The airship rose dead straight, but when it had reached a height of about three hundred feet, it bore to the north—that is, away from the island, and I gathered that the balloon had struck a southerly current.

" Through a megaphone Tatham directed me to steam to the other side of the island. I accordingly got up my anchor and stood out to sea to avoid the reef, and made for the western side, where, as I judged, the air current would be favourable for a landing. We gave the balloon another hundred feet of rope, and this apparently enabled Tatham to secure a bird's-eye view of the island. I gathered that he was pleased with what he saw, for from time to time he shouted down disjointed remarks such as ' Splendid ! ' ' Magnificent ! ' ' Bully ! '

" I need hardly say that I did not regard Captain Tatham's plan for effecting a landing with any degree of confidence. I expected that it would be an arduous and lengthy business. For one thing it was impossible to bring the ship sufficiently close to land to allow the balloon party to throw a line ashore, even if they had means of securing an anchorage. Everything depended upon the air currents, and it seemed for a time as though these were determined to baffle us.

" At the north of the island these were due south, at the west they blew persistently south-east, at the south they canted the balloon in exactly the opposite direction to which the Captain desired. It was when we had returned to our original anchorage that the luck changed, for a current of air caught the little gas-bag and drove it on to the island.

" I took a risk and stood the ship for the shore, paying out another fifty feet of line.

" For a moment it seemed that we failed ; for the fool balloon came swinging back. Then the full force of the breeze caught it, and it was carried over the top of the cliff out of sight. We waited for an anxious ten minutes. Tatham had the tackle to secure the balloon ; all depended upon the wind holding. Apparently it held, for at the end of that period the Captain reappeared and shouting incoherently through his megaphone.

" He had taken up with him a light line and block, and before night came, as it did with a rush, we had managed to pass up blankets and food, a couple of rifles and fifty rounds of ammunition. The next morning we hauled down the balloon, and two more men were sent up. Tatham specially invited Calhus, but the reporter promptly declined to trust his life to the frail machine—which, by the way, needed all the gas we could generate before it consented to rise again.

" The second ascent was not successful, and Tatham gave instructions for a landing to be made on the narrow beach on the north-eastern side of the island. With some difficulty the line was unshipped and re-established on the high cliff overhanging the beach.

" Although our resources were considerably taxed, owing to the shortage of spare gear on the *Scoutina*, by the splicing of lines, and with the assistance of the donkey engine, we hoisted a couple of light spars and other tackle, and on the third day Tatham had fixed up a serviceable derrick capable of bearing the weight of all the equipment he required.

" All this time men were joining the Captain, and after a

week's hard work the hoisting equipment was in capital order. The hardest task of all was getting the donkey engine ashore. I could see this was necessary, for the old arrangement necessitated the use of odds and ends of rope and cable, to complete the enormous length of line required. The donkey engine had to be taken to pieces and sent up in parts—and this meant hand hauling, because Captain Tatham's suggestion that the engines of the ship should be employed, that the propeller should be unshipped and a winding drum fixed in its place, was too impracticable for consideration.

" On the second Sunday following our arrival, in company with Mr. Callus, I paid my first visit to the interior of the island. We were hauled up to the top of the cliff, and Captain Tatham received us."

V

THE EVIDENCE OF THE FOURTH WITNESS : RICHARD CALLUS

Mr. Richard Callus is so well known as a journalist, traveller, and novelist that it would be an impertinence on my part to speak of his claim to credence. He is a man of 37, with a fine nose for a good story and the gift of telling one.

I was fortunate in meeting him, for I arrived in Cadiz after the Tangier boat by which he was passenger (he had been to Casablanca for his paper) had discharged.

I found him in the Café of Four Nations in the Calleo de Recolletos, being directed thereto by his Moorish servant Rabaht, who accompanied him as far as the Spanish city.

Mr. Callus's story is by far the most interesting.

" TATHAM," said Mr. Callus, " looked remarkably pleased with himself, as indeed he had every right to be, in the light of his achievements. Regarded purely from the standpoint of an engineering feat, he had accomplished wonders in establishing communication between the ship and his eyrie.

" To my surprise there was little to be seen from the place where the derrick stood. A further rise of ground hid the interior of the island, and I was walking to this to gratify my curiosity when Tatham stopped me. He so evidently wished to stand in the position of Master of Ceremonies in the introduction that I agreed to defer my sightseeing.

" He had a light lunch prepared for us, a bottle of champagne was opened, and ' Success to Tatham Island ' was most solemnly drunk.

" Then Tatham made the inevitable speech.

"We were, he said, on the threshold of an epoch-making discovery. The land we had spied out was not alone for us, but for posterity. Our children's children, generations yet unborn, should reverence the names of the hardy pioneers who established the flag of freedom in a savage land, who had built a wing to the Empire of Civilisation, and added a storey to the fabric of our glorious possessions. It was very fitting, he said, that a witness to the very act should be a representative of the enlightened press of the United States. He referred to Mr. Callus, a gentleman whose whole-hearted enthusiasm for their great project was in keeping with the splendid traditions of the paper he so ably represented. (He stopped here to ask what was the name of the newspaper, and I answered coldly, ' The War Cry.')

"He went on to deal with problems which had not the remotest connection with our project, Popular Education, Europe's Naval Programme, the future of the Asiatic Races, and the Panama Canal.

"Following the speech came my initiation into the mysteries of the island. That they might come to me with greater force a bandage was folded over my eyes, and I was led to the crest of the ridge which hid the island's interior.

"'Now look !' said Tatham, and whipped off the bandage.

"It was indeed a wonderful scene that he disclosed.

"From my feet the hill sloped gradually to a green valley through which a little river wound : before me rose the tree-covered slopes of the southern 'wall.' Left and right stretched a rolling plain covered, it seemed, with a carpet of flowers.

"Clumps of trees, gorgeous park-like spaces of wood and flowers, a dozen tributary brooks racing to the river, green ribbons of meadowland—veritable rivers of emerald flowing through sombre forests—these were my first impressions of Tatham Island.

"'There's gold there and there and there,' Tatham pointed excitedly. ' I found garnets over by the little brook, and where there are garnets, there are diamonds. And look !—do you see where the river disappears, there's a cave. . . . I'm pretty sure . . . communication with the sea at certain tides : and look at the life, pheasants those fellows, and I saw an oryx this morning. . . .'

"So he pointed from side to side, as a bird flew up, or the flash of a white hide in the valley below attracted him.

"There was reason enough for his enthusiasm. My knowledge of geology is of the slightest, but there was no doubt that this was gold-bearing. At our very feet was evidence of outcrop. Allowing fifty per cent. for Tatham's sanguine temperament this island should prove an Eldorado.

"He had fixed up a rough shelter on the slope of the hill, and he made me comfortable for the night. He told me he had little time to explore the island, and that he had come upon indications of gold without much seeking.

"When I turned in, he came and sat at my side unfolding the most wonderful plans for the future. If the gold turned out as he expected he would people the island with men and women of his own choice. He proposed some remarkable tests for his future citizens. The men must be of a certain age, the women of a certain height. He would have none but grey-eyed men because they could shoot straighter than brown-eyed people. He would require a most exemplary character from the immigrant, and a guarantee deposit of $100 against their misbehaviour. There would be no drink of an intoxicating character imported except for medicinal purposes. He would stock the island with Southdown sheep and Scotch oxen. There would be a city built on the sheltered slope of the northern hill, with electric light and electric traction.

"There should be no coinage, but a check system—a central bank, each citizen being credited with a certain sum monthly according to his usefulness and the amount and importance of the work he accomplished. All houses, roads, electric and water supply should be the common property of the community, and the size of the house apportioned to the applicant would be in strict agreement with his actual requirement. There would be an elaborate system of fortifications on the hills. . . . I'm sorry I did not hear all he said, for I fell asleep in the middle of the recital.

"I was awakened suddenly by an extraordinary noise. At first I thought it was thunder; then in my alarm I diagnosed it earthquake, for I could feel the ground shaking. Tatham, who slept at the other end of the shelter, was on his feet instantly.

"He answered my unspoken query.

"'It's a herd of cattle galloping,' he said; and I instantly recognised the sound.

"'It's strange,' said Tatham, in a puzzled voice. 'I haven't seen a sign of any big herd—what can it be?'

"Not being in the position to answer him I remained silent.

"'I have it,' said Tatham, suddenly. 'Captain Ford refers to a herd of zebra—this must be the zebra.'

"From the tracks we found next morning it was evident that Tatham's deductions were right. It seemed to me, however, that the hoof marks were rather too large for *quagga*. Examining the tracks, I made an extraordinary discovery. On the fringe of the herd there had been apparently one animal by itself.

"The hoof marks were very distinct, especially lower down the hill, where a curious deposit of hard black sand made an excellent record. By great luck, the solitary animal had gone clear across this patch (it wasn't a particularly large one), but to my astonishment there were only three impressions of hoofs. I pointed this out to Tatham.

" ' A three-legged zebra is a monstrosity that must not deface our fair realm,' said Tatham. This was the first time I remember Tatham adopting the curious phraseology peculiar to members of a royal family and editorial leader writers. I thought at first that it was a ponderous piece of humour on his part, and smiled politely at the witticism, but it very soon became apparent that he did in all seriousness regard himself as one of the world's rulers.

" When this attitude became, as it did later, more evident, I was rather struck by Tatham's inconsistency—remembering the outburst of socialism that had marked the ' banquet ' on our landing.

" For the next three days we were all very busy building a settlement. Perhaps Mr. Hackitt made it clear that all supplies from the ship had to be drawn up the face of the cliff by means of an improvised crane. For a long time the difficulty was the actual hauling rope, and when I say that in the earlier stages of our operations some thousand feet of rope was necessary, you will understand the shifts we were put to, to secure the necessary length.

" But with the bringing up of the donkey engine, and the establishment of the motor power on the head of the cliff, haulage became simplified, and the work ran smoothly.

" As this work proceeded, Tatham devoted himself to a tour of inspection, or rather prospection. Accompanied by an old man named Gillett, he tested the various reefs. Such samples of rock as I saw gave me little hope that he would find gold in paying quantities, but Tatham pooh-poohed my doubts. He discoursed learnedly on the eccentricities of gold. How it is found equally in all the sedimentary rocks, from the metamorphic to the post-pliocene beds of tertiary gravels. He talked of diorites, trachytes, of triassic rocks, and calcareous veins till my brain reeled, and he finally left me with the impression that even the cobble-stone is not to be despised as a milling proposition.

" He told me facts about gold that I had never known before ; of gold so finely deposited and of such remarkable thinness, that it floated on water, of gold found in the shape of leaves, so beautiful and fairy-like that they were worth twice their weight-value to collectors ; of ' dead river ' gold ; of seas that washed up auriferous sands from some ghostly gold mine in the ocean's depth.

" He said that he hoped to find extensive alluvial deposits and ' pockets,' because he needed ' quick money.'

" ' The ideal discovery,' he said, ' would be to find rich alluvial beds that might be easily worked, and that would yield me the necessary capital to erect machinery for the recovery of gold from the reef.'

"He took the existence of the reef for granted, and his assurance was rewarded to an extraordinary extent, for on the eighth day he obtained unmistakable evidence of gold.

"From a trench cut in the side of the hill he took a sample of quartz that assayed 30 dwt. Following the supposed direction of the reef he cut another trench some 150 yards away, and made yet another assay, which showed 31.5 pennyweights to the ton. In character the reef was not unlike that of Witwatersrand, and Tatham's men were jubilant. We had a camp-fire concert to celebrate the discovery, and Tatham delivered an address on the Responsibilities of Wealth that lasted an hour and ten minutes, and was listened to with the closest attention by his following.

"They were an extraordinary collection of men. You tell me that Mr. Hackitt has spoken of them as being devoted to Tatham, but this hardly describes the blind faith they had in him. They were not ignorant men, by any means. Two or three of them were University men who had drifted to Rhodesia, had cast aside the trammels of civilisation, and had gone into the wilderness, romantic vagabonds equipped with rifle and prospecting-pan.

"Tatham told me once that he had men from Yale, Princeton, Oxford, Harvard, and Cambridge. Broken men? I do not think they were broken. They were chipped in places, that is all.

"Many of them had spent solitary years in the wilds, shooting a little, digging a little, fighting a little. They had penetrated the untrodden wastes, had bathed in Tanganyika before a railway was dreamt of, had crossed the sandy stretches of the Kalahari, had prospected for gold in the Katanga district, and had un-officially fought the Portuguese in Angola.

"They greatly impressed me by their gift of silence—the desert had taught them that. They had certain physical peculiarities, too. The far-away look that comes into the eyes of men accustomed to the surveying of great distances; the red-brick of sun-scorched faces; the puckering lines about eyes and mouth. I account for none of these characteristics, because I am not learned in the science of physiognomy. I merely place on record the fact that they were a type unto themselves, a well-defined type. In a word they were 'serious.'

"I saw very little evidence of levity, even in face of Tatham's often absurd proposals. Life was an earnest problem to them, and it would appear that there was no inclination to treat it otherwise.

"That there was a humorous side to the expedition cannot be doubted; indeed the whole prospect, viewed in a certain aspect, was grotesquely comic. Tatham's assumptions were Gilbertian;

the stealing of the ship and Captain Tatham's *naïve* justification were alike provocative of laughter.

" But to the men it was all very Napoleonic and big, and they would sooner have chosen the Holy Writ as a subject for their merriment than the Tatham Expedition. With the ' proving ' of the reef came the search for the ' quick money ' alluvial, and it was with the finding of the ' placer ' pocket in Knox's Kloof that there came a crisis in our affairs."

VI

THE EVIDENCE OF THE FOURTH WITNESS : RICHARD CALLUS (*continued*)

Mr. Callus in the course of his interview gave me many particulars which I have not included, since they do not help forward the story, nor are they necessary in a work of this character.

I have verified the statements concerning the wreck of the *Queen of Plata*, and the Bloodstock Agency of England has furnished me with a comprehensive chart which would help to make this chapter of greater interest to the racing man, but I have omitted everything of a technical character, or any details calculated to confuse the non-technical reader.

" I DID not tell you that one of the first things Tatham did on landing was to arrange the geographical nomenclature of the island. Thus we had Taft Hill, Knox's Kloof, the King Edward River, and (I blush to confess) Callus's Heights. The eastern wall was called the Roosevelt Range, the western the Victoria Mountains, the southern the Wilhelmsberg, the northern the Fallier Alps. Tatham said, in all seriousness, that this would prevent international jealousies. Some time afterwards, on the representation of an Australian member of the party, he christened the seaward face of the cliff, up which our stores were drawn, Cape Sydney, and, enamoured with the discovery that there were external features of the island as well as internal, he created a Hackitt Head, Nicholas Point, Alfonso Bay, and his supply of potential royalties running short, he continued with his literary heroes. So we had a James Sound, a Kipling Cove, and a Shakespeare Bluff.

" Knox's Kloof was a little ravine very near the submerged mouth of the King Edward River, and here it was that Tatham found the rich placer deposits that lifted him to the seventh heaven of delight. The gold taken out was almost pure, and in three days nearly a thousand ounces was unearthed—and then the supply ceased as if by magic.

" It was as though some Titanic hand had scooped the precious metal into a big hole, had loosely covered the *cache* with some loose stones and earth, had patted the ground smooth, and had left it for some human delver to unearth. It was far removed from any auriferous reef ; it was unconnected with any alluvial deposit, pocketed in an unlikely spot by Nature's mysterious agency, its very presence betokened a puzzle set by an Omniscient Providence for the bewilderment of man.

" With feverish energy Tatham dug, probed, and explored. The pocket was exhausted. Far into that night we searched by the light of fires, and as soon as dawn came we were at it again, but without success. Tatham, however, did not lose heart. His contention was that if we had found one pocket by accident, there were dozens, perhaps hundreds, of others to be discovered by search.

" It seemed a feasible argument, but there is no logic in chance. We were up against one of Nature's inscrutable jests, for search as we did, in the most likely, and the most unlikely spots, no gold could we find. I can dismiss in four words the history of the next fortnight—we sought gold unsuccessfully.

" Gold there was in the rocks, of course, but it was not the ' quick money ' we looked for.

" More and more obvious it became to me, that upon the finding of a rich deposit depended the issue of the expedition. Mining machinery is expensive, and there were other considera-tions, the victualling of the party, and the purchase of the equip-ment which was to place Tatham's Utopian kingdom upon a sound basis. In saying this, I am regarding the situation through Tatham's eyes.

" From my point of view there was no reason why he and his party should not have put in a couple of years' solid labour, working the reef with the primitive means at hand, and roughing it, as most of the party were evidently used to roughing it. So far as provisions went, there was plenty of game on the island, and the seed and roots he had brought with him from Loanda already showed signs of healthy growth. But that was not Tatham's way.

" He volunteered the superfluous information that he was a big man with big ideas, and that it was whole hog or nothing with him. Accordingly the search for the phantom pocket continued.

" It was on one of the excursions made in this quest, the last, as a matter of fact, that we made an extraordinary discovery.

" Our temporary quarters were on the side of the Roosevelt Range, and our explorations had mainly been directed along the base of these hills, and in a westerly direction (flanking Wilhelmsberg towards Knox's Kloof). So practically we had not crossed the river, which at Knox's Kloof is some fifty feet wide. Tatham decided to continue his prospecting along the timbered slopes of the Victoria Mountains as far as Taft's Hill, and that morning we accordingly struck inland, intending to cross the river, and following it to its mouth, work systematically north. It was a more difficult task than we had supposed, for the river is fed by numerous racing tributaries, all of which had to be negotiated, and a search for a ford in the river itself took us the greater part of one morning. I must claim credit for finding it, for accidentally I came upon the tracks of the zebra-like creatures to which I have already referred, and these led us to the water's edge at a spot which looked particularly uninviting.

" However, we made the attempt.

" The water ran smoothly and without a ripple to suggest hidden rocks or shallowness, but to our surprise there was no difficulty in the fording, except that of preserving a balance against the swift current.

" It seems at this point the river flows over a huge rock, the width of the river's bed. Æons of friction have rendered the surface of this rock as smooth as pebble, and we forded the stream in comparative comfort. I had brought my rifle with me in the hope of getting a shot at the game we knew was to be found on this bank, and I had the satisfaction of bowling over a little antelope, not unlike the *bles-bok* of South Africa. We marked the spot so that we might pick it up on our return, and proceeded.

" After tramping two miles we struck a beautifully level stretch of grass land that ran due west to the very foot of Taft's Hill. Thereupon Tatham decided to abandon the river and to strike across country to the hill. I have spoken of the park-like beauty of the island.

" From the mountain this is impressive enough, but close at hand the similitude is manifest. Dotted here and there were clumps of beautiful trees. Some of these were of a semi-tropical nature, box-wood, and a tree that I have seen in Central Africa (the Ingola, I think, it is called), a species of pine (Copal), oak, eucalyptus, and the common fir.

" There were also a few rubber plants or what looked like rubber plants, although when I made an incision in the stems with my knife they did not ' bleed,' as would the true caoutchouc (*Siphonia elastica*).

" We did not make the progress we had intended because our attention was being so constantly diverted by the beauties of the scene. Indeed, we dawdled through that wonderful strip of grassland as country cousins dawdle along Broadway, a prey to the attractions of every new shop window.

" Tatham saw a bird running through the grass to the shelter of a friendly covert, and insisted that it was a peacock. This led to our stalking it. We followed it into the cool recesses of one of the little copses. I believe it must have hidden in a dense patch of undergrowth, but I have no clear recollection of what happened to the bird, for Tatham suddenly stopped and looked down.

" I was some distance from him, with Hackitt, who was one of our party, a little ahead.

" ' Come here,' said Tatham quickly ; and I ran back, thinking that perchance the long-looked-for ' pocket ' had been unearthed. I found Tatham gazing at a skeleton. It was the skeleton of an animal.

" ' If that is zebra,' said Tatham, ' we have struck upon the biggest kind of zebra that has ever been discovered.'

" He stood watching the white bones intently ; then he said—

" ' If this wasn't Tatham Island I should say we'd found the skeleton of a horse.'

" Hackitt stooped down and picked up a hoof, and Tatham gasped.

" ' Shod ! ' he said, and truly it was.

" We looked at another.

" ' Shod ! ' repeated Tatham slowly. ' Look at the plate.'

" I looked.

" ' Look at the type of shoe,' said Tatham.

" I must confess that the fact that we should find the remains of a shod horse on this island was more remarkable than the variety of shoe it wore.

" Beyond the fact that the steel tip looked too fragile for rough wear, I saw nothing extraordinary in it. I told him so, and he smiled mysteriously.

" ' I want to think,' he said, and sat down on the soft carpet of pine needles, with his head between his hands.

" He sat like this for the greater part of half an hour, until in my impatience I suggested a move.

" ' The only thing this proves,' I said, ' is that somebody has been here before us, but how they got the horse ashore, heaven only knows.'

" He arose slowly, shaking his head.

" ' We will go and look for those zebras,' he said.

" ' You don't think they are *horses* ? ' I said in astonishment.

" ' I do,' said Tatham firmly ; ' in fact, I am sure.'

" It was remarkable that since we were awakened that night by the thunder of their hoofs we had not caught a glimpse of the herd, a fact that I had previously commented upon, but which Tatham explained by pointing out how easy it would be for such animals as we thought they were to keep out of sight.

"After finding the horse's remains, we gave up our gold-search and concentrated our attention on the herd. We found their spoor easily enough. It led to the right of Taft Hill, through the thick woods at the foot of the 'Alps' (there was a well-defined path through the forest) to a little 'shelf' on the foothills. We came upon them suddenly. I suppose there were seventy in all, and magnificent creatures they were.

"We sighted them through the thicket and moved cautiously towards them.

"'Zebras!' whispered Tatham derisively.

"And well might he be derisive, for never have I seen such a beautiful collection of horses in a perfectly wild state.

"These were of all ages. A big, bony stallion, great up-standing mares with foals at foot, yearlings rough of coat and awkwardly built, young horses with coats that shone like satin.

"'For the Lord's sake!' whispered Tatham, in an ecstasy of admiration, 'look at that fellow! Look at the bone and the heart-room! Did you ever see such quarters? Look at that young mare——'

"So he whispered fiercely in my ear till one of the herd flung up his head and neighed. Instantly there was a wild stampede. Like a flash the herd thundered past us, through the wood and out of sight.

"All save one. The big, bony stallion. He stood with his ears pricked facing us, and Tatham stepped out of his place of concealment and walked towards him with outstretched arm. He was a born horse lover, and the old stallion limped un-hesitatingly towards him and nuzzled his hand.

"Tatham stroked his neck and murmured the unintelligible sounds of encouragement that man uses to his familiar beast.

"Tatham looked round triumphantly as we followed him.

"'Did you ever know a wild horse to do that?' he asked, and, without waiting for an answer, he went on: 'This fellow has met men before, though I doubt whether the others have.'

"He bent down and lifted the horse's forefoot.

"'He's been shod, too,' he said; then, to me, 'How old do you think this beast is?'

"I hazarded a guess.

"'Twenty years.'

"Tatham smiled.

"'I think I can tell you within a year or so. He's thirty-four.'

" He had wrenched the plate from the hoof of the skeleton we had found, and now produced it from his pocket.

" ' Look here,' he said, and indicated what appeared to be three letters hammered into the steel. They were almost indecipherable, but I saw an ' M ' and an ' S.' The centre letter I could not make out. It might have been an ' R ' or a ' B.'

" ' It is a " P," ' said Tatham, calmly, ' and the three letters are " M.P.S." ' He waited for us to seize upon the solution, but I am afraid I was dense.

" ' And what does " M.P.S." mean ? ' I asked.

" ' Middle Park Stud,' said Tatham. ' There was a vessel wrecked——'

" ' The *Queen of Plata* ! ' I cried. ' She had racehorses on board, but——'

" ' There is no *but*,' said Tatham ; ' these are, sure enough, thoroughbreds—racehorses.'

" He held up the rusty plate again.

" ' This is a racing plate : I recognized it instantly.'

" ' But it is impossible,' I objected. ' How could they have got ashore ? There is no way into the island except by climbing the cliff.'

" ' I'm not so sure of that,' said Tatham ; ' in fact, the presence of these horses proves the contrary. I've more than a belief that the river is the explanation. That at certain seasons of the year there is a clear passage from the sea by means of the tunnel.'

" He patted the old horse, and we turned to go.

" ' We'll rope a few of these fellows,' he said ; ' they'll be of splendid service to us. At present,' he went on, ' it is rather too early to form the Tatham Island Turf Club.' He said this quite seriously, and returned to the subject when an hour later we were walking through the grassland.

" ' This is where the track will be,' he said. ' We will run it on a Pari-Mutuel basis with a yearly dividend for all concerned. . . . The State shall take ten per cent.——'

" By the time we had got back to camp he had decided upon the conditions of the Tatham Island Derby.

" The ' roping ' of the horses, of which Tatham spoke so airily, was a tedious business. Expert as many of his men were in the art of lassoing, they found their game very shy and unapproachable. Tatham had marked out six of the younger horses, and one of the elder, a wonderfully proportioned creature, for capture. The older horse was the first one caught, and all mining operations were suspended during the process.

" The last three were roped, after a roughly constructed trap had been built, into which the affrighted animals were driven. The task of breaking them in was handed over to two men, Summers, and a tall wiry man who was called 'The Prince,' from what cause I have never been able to discover. Tatham had chosen his men well, for in an extraordinarily short space of time the animals were tractable and well behaved, and the first indication I had of the success of the training was to see 'The Prince' cantering bare-backed across the grassland with Tatham, stop-watch in hand, a critical spectator.

"We spent another fortnight in fruitless and profitless search for gold, and when Tatham told me that he intended calling a meeting of the men to discuss the situation, I knew that his plans must have undergone a change.

"'By the way,' he said, 'do you remember our three-legged zebra?'

"I laughed.

"'Yes—we haven't found the horse that made those tracks.'

"He nodded.

"'Yes, we have—at least, I think I have; it's the bay.'

"He referred to the older horse we had roped.

"'But he is sound enough,' I said.

"'He's sound enough,' said Tatham quietly, 'but he made those tracks.'

"'But how do you account for them?' I asked.

"'I account for them by his stride,' said Tatham; 'he's an exceptionally far-striding horse. I've been measuring some of his tracks to-day. We galloped him on the sand by the river; only three of his feet touched that path.'

"Beyond the natural feeling of interest in the explanation of the 'three-legged zebra,' Tatham's remark did not suggest anything unusual to me, and I forgot all about it. The meeting of the men had been called for the hour following that of the evening meal, and standing with his back to the fire that had been lighted, Tatham made his speech.

"It was to all intents and purposes a Presidential address.

"Without saying as much, or in so many words, Tatham suggested that our foreign relations were of the friendliest character, and the prospects brighter than the Noonday Sun. He dealt with the events of the past month, of how 'We acquired the necessary sea transport,' of how in 'face of almost insuperable difficulties we had effected a landing on these beneficent shores.'

"A remarkable mixture of President's Inaugural address, King's speech, and director's yearly report.

"'We feel that it is our duty,' Tatham proceeded soberly,

' to place before you the exact position, particularly in regard to our financial standing.' He drew a rough estimate of the sums required for the carrying out of his scheme.

" ' We have earmarked a $125,000 for machinery, $60,000 for portable dwellings, $40,000 for armaments, $25,000 for the upkeep and equipment of our fleet, *The Scoutina*, $50,000 for stores and maintenance, making a total of $300,000.

" He then let us into the secret.

" ' In the course of prospecting we have discovered on the northern slopes of Taft's Hill surface indications of coal, a discovery of inestimable importance.'

" He went on to deal with the present condition of our exchequer.

" ' We have discovered gold to the extent of $17,500, and so far this forms the full sum of our monetary assets. But,' he continued, and I noticed an odd thrill in his voice, ' we have, at a critical period in our career, found a most precious treasure.'

" He paused dramatically, and you could hear the breathing of his audience.

" ' We have found,' he went on, ' a horse that can gallop a mile and a half in 2 minutes 35 seconds.'

" A wondering murmur greeted this statement.

" ' When we tell you,' said Tatham impressively, ' that it took Flying Fox 2 minutes 42 seconds, and Persimmon the same time, and the mighty Ormonde 3 seconds longer ; when you know that Shotover took 2 minutes 45 seconds to win the Derby, and Bend Or 2 minutes 46 seconds, you will realize how tremendous, how epoch-making, is this discovery of ours.'

" ' We need hardly say that we intend exploiting this discovery.' A whole-hearted cheer rounded the sentence, and prevented Tatham's voice from being heard for the time.

" ' Owing to impending legislation in our own fair country, legislation tending to the destruction of a noble sport, I cannot afford the United States an opportunity for seeing the performances of the world's equine wonder.

" ' But the racing season is in full swing in England,' he added. ' To England we will go. We shall take with us every cent we possess ; we shall take with us The Fighting Scout, for such we have named our horse. You may be assured that we shall not return empty-handed.'

" There was a perfect hurricane of cheering as he finished.

" I must confess that I was carried away by the general enthusiasm, although this newest and most freakish of Tatham's schemes took my breath away.

" ' You will find extraordinary difficulties,' I pointed out, as soon as I could get near to him—for he was surrounded by a throng of eager, questioning men, who for the first time cast away all restraint and reserve.

" ' I know that,' he said, ' and I am quite prepared for the difficulties.'

" ' Do you know anything about the Rules of British Racing ? ' I asked.

" He produced from his pocket a well-thumbed copy of a sporting book. I think it was ' Racing-Up-to-Date,' issued by the *Sporting Chronicle*, of Manchester.

" ' Here is the only clause that affects me,' he said, and read out—

" ' 69. A horse foaled out of the United Kingdom shall not be qualified to start for any race until there have been a deposit at the Registry Office, and a fee of 5s. paid on each certificate, (1) such a foreign certificate, and (2) such a certificate of age as are next mentioned, that is to say : The foreign certificate must state the age, sex, pedigree and colour of the horse and any mark by which it may be distinguished, and must be signed by the secretary of some approved racing club of the country in which the horse was foaled, or by some magistrate, mayor or public officer of that country . . . the certificate of age must be signed by a veterinary surgeon.'

" ' As chief magistrate of Tatham Island,' said Tatham coolly, ' I shall of course render the necessary certificate. As for the " vet."—why, half a dozen of our men have *that* diploma.'

" With Tatham to think out a scheme was to carry it into execution, and the following morning began the process of embarkation.

" It was typical of his knowledge of men, that he called for volunteers, not to take the risk of a journey to England, but to remain behind in charge of the island.

" There were ten volunteers, most of them being elderly men, and to the leader of these Tatham confided the scheme of work that was to be carried out in his absence. Short as was the time at his disposal, the table of directions that we drew up were elaborate in detail and covered sixteen sheets of foolscap.

" We embarked on the 10th of May, without incident. A specially constructed sling was used to lower the horse.

" His head was carefully hooded, and he reached the deck of the *Scoutina* without mishap. It was during the lowering that I saw on Tatham's face, for the first and only time, indications of fear and anxiety. He stood on the bridge with two little semaphore flags directing the engineer at the head of the cliff, and when the horse was gently lowered—almost inch by inch in the last dozen yards—he breathed deep like a man from whose mind had rolled the weight of the world's care.

"With The Fighting Scout safely boxed, we signalled *au revoir* to the island and to the men—pigmy figures they made as they stood on the brow of the cliff—and stood away north for England."

VII

THE EVIDENCE OF THE FOURTH WITNESS :
RICHARD CALLUS (*continued*)

Supporting this third section of Mr. Callus's evidence I have a report from a trusted correspondent in Villa Nova de Milfontes (Portugal), a statement very kindly forwarded by the editor of the *Sporting Chronicle* and copies of estimates and specifications furnished by the Hilsome Traders Machinery Co., the Elswick Gun Manufactory, and other firms of repute. Since they merely confirm all that Mr. Callus says, it is inexpedient to produce their evidence in detail.

"AFTER the discomforts of the island life, discomforts inseparable in the very nature of things from the adventure, I was pleased to get back to my comfortable berth on the *Scoutina*, more especially as two nights before our sailing a heavy shower had not only soaked me, but had also reached my reserve stock of clothing, and I was prepared to face the dangers of starvation in exchange for a comfortable bed.

"When I speak of starvation, I refer to our shortage of provisions. Tatham had very rightly insisted upon most generous supplies being apportioned to the men we had left behind, and accordingly we were on two-thirds rations from the very beginning of the voyage. If this fact had been kept from us instead of being paraded at every meal we might not have noticed it.

"But with the consciousness of a dearth of provisions, one's appetite increased in inverse ratio to the food supply. The catering left much to be desired, and only one passenger could truthfully claim to retire nightly, pleasantly full—and that was The Fighting Scout.

"He was fed regally and regularly.

"Tatham, bringing his mind down to the consideration of an ideal diet for racehorses, would have made sundry dietary experiments on the horse, but against this 'The Prince,' who was the custodian of our treasure, most resolutely set his face.

" ' No, Ned,' he said firmly, when Tatham approached the subject. ' I'm no believer in giving condensed milk to horses of any kind—but to a racehorse most decidedly and emphatically " No " ! '

" Captain Tatham did evolve a system of physical exercise for racehorses, and somewhat reluctantly ' The Prince ' agreed to a trial of this. There was very little exercise the horse could get, save to and fro in the tiny well-deck of the ship. Tatham's Horse Exerciser was an ingenious arrangement of barrels and planks that made a moving platform, the motive power being the horse himself. It did not work.

" Undismayed by the failure, he then invented ' spring-pads.' These consisted of four stout copper springs, one for each foot. They were faced and backed with discs of wood, and the idea was to strap them to the unfortunate animal's feet. Providing he stood perfectly still, the swaying of the ship would exercise on each leg alternately a gentle upward pressure that could not fail to be vastly beneficial to the tendons and muscles of each leg so treated.

" As The Fighting Scout was not a circus horse, and generally lacked the necessary training, this scheme was also abandoned. But for the excitement engendered by these experiments the voyage was eventless. On the 25th of May we sighted the sugar-loaf cone of Teneriffe, and gave it a wide berth. Hackitt estimated that our coal would last us as far as London if we decided to enter the Kingdom by way of the Thames. Of course, Tatham had decided upon London as the port offering least chance of detection.

" I had no doubt that the story of the stolen ship was pretty generally known and port officials would be on the look-out for us. I knew, too, that the thought of this danger was ever present in Tatham's mind. There would be a difficulty about ship's papers, too, that I could not see how he was to overcome, but I reckoned without the supreme resourcefulness of the man.

" When I mentioned the matter to him, he said that he had an invariable rule, formed when a member of the Border Police which patrols the three frontiers of Angola. ' When in doubt, play Portugal.' I was not surprised, therefore, when we were three days clear of the Canaries that he stood in for the Portuguese coast.

" Just after the sunset gun had been fired, we dropped anchor in the roadstead of Villa Nova de Milfontes. Since it was after sunset, we were not boarded by the customs officers or harbour officials, and we were accordingly prohibited from landing.

" But port regulations would have little deterrent effect upon Tatham, and as soon as it was dark he had a boat lowered and was rowed ashore.

" I, personally, cannot imagine what argument Captain Tatham could have used to induce the officials to allow him to land. He had a command of flowery Portuguese, but this would hardly be sufficient passport. The suggestion of bribery is out of place, and one which Tatham himself would have instantly rejected, for he took a very serious view concerning the probity of the public services.

" The only thing I am certain about is, that he went ashore, that he remained ashore until three o'clock on the following morning, that he came back looking very thoughtful and gave orders to Hackitt to put to sea.

" To me, he delivered himself of a few cryptic utterances on the Decadence of Nations, the Corrupting Influences of Gold, together with a short homily defending the Jesuits from the charge of having laid down the dictum that the end justified the means.

" After which he went to bed.

" Next day the *Scoutina* became the *San Maria de Sines*, and when we passed a British man-o'-war in the Bay we dipped a Portuguese flag to her.

" It was on the 3rd of June that we rounded the Nore lightship and entered the Thames. I was quite prepared for the scene that followed the arrival of the inspection officers.

" Captain Tatham, taking the position of skipper, produced his papers, said a few complimentary nothings in broken English, swore volubly at the steersman in fluent Portuguese, and bidding a smiling farewell to the port officials, brought the ship slowly up the Thames with an unsuspecting pilot endeavouring to hold a conversation with Hackitt in bad Portuguese—much to that gentleman's embarrassment.

" In the privacy of his cabin Tatham informed me that we were the *San Maria de Sines* out of Cercal in ballast, and as such we came to our moorings in the Pool.

" Up to now everything had gone swimmingly, almost too swimmingly, in fact, for I am of opinion that Providence holds something particularly unpleasant for the man who draws two to a flush, twice in succession.

" Had I been Tatham, I should have been alarmed by my easy success, but Tatham was not the kind of man to be alarmed at anything. With his permission I went ashore immediately, for my private affairs by this time would need a little adjusting. I did not expect that anybody would be greatly alarmed by my absence, for I was supposed to be in the Congo (not, as Mr. Hackitt said, Angola) and consequently beyond all outside communication.

" The editor of my paper was mildly pleased to see me back

again ; mildly interested in the result of my investigations, and perfectly willing, when I pointed out that I had the biggest kind of ' story ' under weigh, to allow me further time to develop it.

" I dined that night at the Lamb's Club, played a rubber or two at bridge, then wandered into the Strand to give myself over to the joy of seeing and hearing and smelling one of the few cities in the world where life is worth living.

" Early next morning I went down to the Pool, to find that Tatham had secured a berth at Sigley's Wharf—the appendage to a ramshackle array of wooden warehouses on the Surrey side.

" By the time I reached the ship The Fighting Scout was ashore. Accommodation had been found in the stables of the British Lion, a public-house facing the wharf. Tatham, when I got to the public-house, was orating the bar-tender on the care of thoroughbreds. The man listened attentively, but wholly uncomprehending.

" A room had been found for ' The Prince,' who was to have charge of the horse, and it was arranged that the next day, suitable training quarters should be found for the Hope of Tatham Island.

" Before anything else could be done, however, our gold had to be disposed of—the placer gold we had brought with us. Securing—with some difficulty—a four-wheeled cab, we drove to the Bank of England, and here, the proper official having been found, the gold was handed over for assay and purchase. I did not know until then that the Bank of England is compelled to buy all gold that is offered to it.

" Tatham took his receipt for the bullion and arranged to return on the following day for the cash value. We then went on to my bank in Fleet Street (I find it useful to have an account in Europe), where for the first time in my impecunious career I found a substantial balance to my credit. I was able to finance Tatham to the extent of a hundred and fifty pounds. It may be as well to say here that Tatham's cash in hand amounted to about fifteen dollars, the remains of that identical forty dollars which, as he told Hackitt, formed his capital.

" From the bank we went on to Messrs. Weatherby's in Old Bond Street. Here we got a copy of the Racing Calendar, and a list of Races to Close. We were also afforded an interview with one of the firm's representatives, a most courteous gentleman who gave us a great deal of very useful information.

" Tatham stated that he was a ' colonel ' domiciled at Hope Island, and expressed his desire to register his horse. He described the horse as a bay colt, 4 years old, with a white blazed face. As for pedigree, he said both the dam and sire were un-known, that the horse had been found wandering, had been caught by him, and finding that he ' went a bat ' (I use Tatham's own words), he had trained him.

" ' I shall make no complaint,' he orated, ' if the handi-cappers allot him the weight of a first-class horse—for such I believe him to be.'

" He then produced the requisite certificates which were duly registered, and entered The Fighting Scout for half a dozen races that had yet to close, including a selling race at Windsor, the Cesarewitch, the Portland Handicap at Doncaster, a mile selling race at Kempton Park, and a Five Furlong Sprint at Lingfield.

" The official smiled when he read the entries.

" ' You have some faith in the versatility of your horse, Mr. Deane ' (this was the name Tatham used).

" ' Why ? ' asked Tatham.

" ' Well,' smiled the gentleman, ' you have entered him for the races over 5, 6, and 7 furlongs, a mile, a mile and a half, and one of two miles and a quarter ! '

" ' He is a remarkable horse,' said Tatham, gravely.

" ' I can well imagine so,' said the official, politely.

" Walking down Bond Street, Tatham enlarged on the ethics of racing.

" Since I am racing under a false name, I suppose I am liable to all kinds of disqualifications,' he said. ' I have even made false statements in regard to the circumstance of my coming into possession of the horse. Nevertheless, I desire to race honestly ; I have given my opinion as to the merits of the horse, an opinion that will be confirmed by its running.'

" ' I suppose you know,' I pointed out, ' that by putting a horse in a selling race you run a great risk of losing him ? '

" ' By running him,' corrected Tatham, ' not by entering him. It remains to be seen what our plans of campaign will be. In the meantime I have other important and urgent matters to settle. Chief of these is the question of racing colours. What do you say to purple and gold, scarlet sleeves, black cap ? '

" I looked him straight in the eye. It was the only time I had ever caught him at a disadvantage.

" ' Those colours are already registered by the King of England,' I said coldly.

" Eventually he chose ' Emerald green with white spots, cerise cap and cuffs.'

" I did not see Tatham the next day until three o'clock in the afternoon, when we met by appointment at my club.

" The sale of the gold had been satisfactorily carried out,

he informed me, and he had received the sum of £3878 12s. 4d., about $19,000. He repaid me the sum I had advanced him, and told me that he had secured excellent quarters for The Fighting Scout at Epsom.

"It appears that there was a very first-class trainer there who at the moment had a number of empty boxes. The trainer's name was Holton. Tatham was enthusiastic concerning the capability and acumen of the trainer, no less than with his discretion. By judicious inquiry I discovered that the main evidence of the trainer's sagacity lay in the fact that he agreed with all the extraordinary views that Tatham put forward on the training and care of racehorses.

"He may have trained for owners of the Tatham type before.

"I learnt, too, that the trainer had found quarters for 'The Prince,' and that, if the preliminary gallops were satisfactory, and The Fighting Scout went well in training, he was to run in the Park Mile Selling Handicap at Windsor.

"As I had already pointed out to Tatham, there is a considerable danger in running a good horse in a selling race. The conditions of the race are simply explained. It is usually 'a race for $500, the winner to be sold for $500.' This means that if his horse wins, it is to be put up to auction on the spot, and the owner may, if he wishes, 'buy in.'

"The danger is not so much in winning as in losing, for the owners of horses who finish in front of him may 'claim' him. That is, by depositing $1000—$500 the value of the stake, and $500 the advertised selling price—he or they may take the horse from your possession willy-nilly.

"Tatham scoffed at the idea of The Fighting Scout being beaten, although I assailed his ears with stories of horses regarded as unbeatable which had come to grief in selling races.

"It was abhorrent to his nature, he said, to contemplate catastrophe. I got an opportunity of asking Mr. Holton his private opinion of The Fighting Scout.

"'He's the most wonderful horse I've ever seen,' he said simply. 'I'm not saying this to please you, but because I shouldn't be doing the horse justice if I said less. I took him out on the Downs the morning after he arrived and galloped him with Careless Lady—*she* won the Victoria Cup under 112—and your horse simply lost her. I saw the gallop and rated the lad who was up on the filly for not going fast enough, but he said the Lady was putting in every ounce she had.'

"'Isn't it a mistake to run The Scout in a selling race?' I asked; but the diplomatic trainer shrugged his shoulders.

"'I've seen greater mistakes made,' he said. 'As I understand it, Mr. Deane ' (I forgot for the moment Tatham's *nom de course*) ' is out for a gamble, and I must confess I have seen few better gambling media.'

" The ship by this time had been handed over to a ' ship's-husband,' and Tatham's men, by common consent, had migrated to Epsom.

" I do not know that I have seen a spectacle that has more impressed me than that which accompanied The Scout's morning gallop. It was usually fixed for seven o'clock, and an hour before that time you might see little knots of men, in twos and threes and singly, making their way across the sun-bathed downs to the appointed place.

" They would dispose of themselves in a skeleton line that ran the whole length of the gallop and wait silently and solemnly till the sheeted figure of the great stallion made his appearance.

" In a sense it was pathetic, nay, it was tragic, for on the exertions of this long-striding horse depended a wondrous future. If it be remembered, too, that they had elected to live on something like three dollars a week in order that every penny of their capital should go to the support of The Scout in the betting ring, and that Tatham was denying himself of every luxury, living in cheap lodgings off Waterloo Road with the same object, you may comprehend to some extent the fervent earnestness of these men and their doggedness of purpose.

" I was curious to see what the newspapers—that is, the sporting newspapers—said of The Scout. From my point of view, as well as from the trainer's, the less that was said about him the better. But Tatham's annoyance, when he read in the ' Training Reports ' that ' Holton was out this morning with a new arrival that galloped like a hack,' was so intense, that it was only with the greatest difficulty that we restrained him from writing an insulting letter to the editor.

" Thus we read—

" ' Holton's string took gentle exercise. The Scout went short in his gallop, and is evidently no flier.'

" And—

" ' Careless Lady led The Scout a good mile canter at half speed. Careless Lady is deteriorating, for she had all her work cut out to show the way to such a second-class horse as The Scout.'

" And on the day before the race—

" ' The best of ours for the Park Mile Selling is JOHN-BERRY. The Fighting Scout is also engaged, but may be safely passed over.'

" ' Excellent,' said the trainer, rubbing his hands, and smiling into Tatham's troubled face. ' We couldn't have a better report.'

" ' I'm not so sure,' said Tatham, ' that I cannot sue these people for libel—they are depreciating the value of the horse.'

" The trainer laughed.

" ' There are many owners who would welcome such a depreciation,' he said drily.

" On the way to Windsor he gave us a curious insight into the mysteries of the turf.

" ' The racing public are at once the most credulous and the most suspicious people in the world,' he said ; ' they believe little of what they are told, and less of what they see. A public trial of horses under their very eyes they promptly ignore, but does some ragged little boy whisper a rumour of a midnight test, they will trample one another to death in their anxiety to back the mythical trial winner.'

" We reached Windsor an hour before racing started, and lunched at an hotel near the station. Tatham had brought with him a thousand pounds in notes, and half this sum he handed to ' The Prince,' with instructions to dole it out amongst the men. The idea was that it would be easier to place in small sums than in one large amount.

" Tatham, with his love for organisation, had worked out the whole scheme. At a signal from him, ten men would simultaneously approach the ten biggest bookmakers in Tattersall's and take the best odds procurable to fifty pounds. He himself would endeavour to secure the odds to a ' monkey '—$2500.

" The meeting could not have been chosen with greater intelligence, for it was the Saturday following the Ascot Meeting, when owners and trainers were out to recover their losses—it had been a disastrous Ascot for backers—and money would be free, and gambling very heavy.

" Holton said that to his knowledge there were six horses in The Scout's race that would be heavily supported. This promised well. We had yet to secure a jockey, and with the possibility of big fields, it looked as though we might experience some difficulty in obtaining the services of a first-class man. As a precautionary measure, Holton had brought one of his own apprentice lads.

" ' Most of the American boys will be engaged,' he said, pointing to his race card. ' Biggs will ride that, Maher will ride that, Malsey will be up on that thing of Hunt's, Madden will ride that, Trigg that—all Hallick's boys will be engaged—we shall have to take our chance.'

" We arrived on the course just before the first race, and Holton went in search of a jockey. We strolled into the paddock to get a glimpse of The Fighting Scout. He was walking quietly round the ring under the charge of ' The Prince ' and a stable lad. I do not suppose, in the long and romantic history of horse-racing, there was ever a ' plater ' who carried on his back such responsibility or whose success or failure would be fraught with such consequences more vital. I had now reached a stage where the humour of the situation failed to amuse me. No heart beat faster than mine in anticipation of this coming struggle. I almost agreed with the magniloquent claim of Tatham, that the issue before us was an ' Imperial issue.'

" I saw Holton walking quickly towards us, talking to a little man at his side.

" ' This is Mr. Plant, Mr. Deane,' he said, with every evidence of satisfaction. ' Plant is disengaged for the race, so I have given him the mount on The Scout.'

" I looked down into the quizzical features of this famous light-weight, and wished we could take him into our confidence ; that we could tell him everything that depended on his efforts. He was a cheery little man, stoutly and strongly built, a veritable ' Pocket Hercules '—such, I believe, is his nick-name.

" He walked over to The Scout and looked at him carefully.

" ' Can he go ? ' he asked, and the trainer nodded.

" ' They think,' Plant jerked his hand back towards the weighing-room, ' that Applescrap is a certainty.'

" ' So much the better,' said Holton.

" Tatham here interposed.

" ' I should like to give you a few hints about riding this horse,' he said, and proceeded to lay down the law on the art of race riding, with some remarks upon the American seat, and the judgment of pace.

" To Plant's credit, it must be said that he listened with every indication of interest. Once or twice I detected a strangled yawn, but Tatham was so engrossed in his exposition, that they passed unnoticed. In the end, Plant went away to weigh-out for the third race. We did not leave the paddock. Three times we heard the thunder of horses' hoofs, and the swelling roar from the rings. Three times a sweating horse, lathered white, was led to the ring ; three times a stentorian voice roared ' All—Ri-i-ight ! '

" Then came Plant, resplendent in ' emerald green and white spots, cerise cuffs and cap,' and the sheet was stripped from The Fighting Scout. The stirrup leathers were adjusted, and the little man hoisted into the saddle, with his knees bunched up over the horse's withers, and the reins gathered in his hands.

" We got back to the ring, and waited for the field to canter past.

"I thought The Scout's action was faulty; he seemed to gallop a little short, but Tatham did not appear to be greatly alarmed.

"There was a perfect furore for Applescrap. Even money was offered in places, but generally the fielders were taking a stand of odds. It was 'Six to one bar one,' the second favourite being Malina, a grey filly by Grey Leg.

"Tatham delayed his signal until the market was settled— then he gave it. 'Get what odds you can for yourself,' he said hurriedly, then stepped down into the ring.

"I strolled off to the outskirts of the crowd, and took 200 to 14 twice.

"A little later I saw 'The Prince' taking twelve ponies twice ($3000 to $250).

"Tatham, I learnt afterwards, had been singularly fortunate, considering he was investing $2500 in one sum.

"There was a long delay at the post, and this gave us time to compare notes. Tatham was for some unaccountable reason chagrined to find that on the strength of his investments, The Scout had not become a sound favourite. As a matter of fact, it had come down the list with a run, opening at a 100 to 6, and closing firm at 7 to 1. Such was the openness of the market that had we the money with us, another two thousand pounds might have been invested without appreciably altering the price. We were discussing the possibility when there was a roar, 'They're off!'

"They came into sight round the bend, and I looked in vain for the cerise cap.

"I heard Tatham mutter an oath and the trainer at my side swear softly.

"'Good Lord! he's left!' he muttered.

"I looked carefully through my glasses, but there was no cerise cap, and my heart sank.

"'Applescrap is making the running,' said the trainer, 'with something in a dark cap lying second and going like the devil.'

"Up the straight they swept, a glittering patchwork of brightly coloured silk.

"'The favourite's beaten!' said the trainer.

"I looked back, still no sign of The Scout.

"'The brute!'

"Then at my side, a calm racing reporter dictated to a scribbling *confrère*: 'At the distance Applescrap was beaten, and something in green with white spots—he's lost his cap somewhere—went on——'

"'The Scout wins!' yelled Tatham, and the green jacket went under the wire like a flash.

"I believe that in his exuberance Tatham would have made

a speech to the ring, but we hurried him down to the sales ring. Plant was dismounting as we got there.

" ' I'd like to know the man who invented the cap I wore,' he said wrathfully. ' It had a spring or something in it, for as soon as the gate went up, up went the cap too.'

" Tatham coughed ; he was slightly embarrassed.

" ' The idea was mine,' he said ; ' it struck me that the type of cap might be improved by the addition of a spring that would firmly fix it to the head of the wearer.'

" Plant smiled sardonically, and carried his saddle into the weighing room.

" The cry of ' All right ' brought me to a realisation of our victory.

" ' My best congratulations, Tatham ! ' I said heartily, ' first blood——'

" The auctioneer's voice broke in on my felicitations.

" ' Here we have The Fighting Scout, a winner,' he said, ' dam and pedigree unknown, but none the worse for that ; who'll start me at a hundred ? '

" He got a start soon enough, and for a few minutes the bidding steadily mounted.

" ' Two hundred guineas I'm offered—and fifty.'

" ' Two hundred and fifty guineas I'm offered.'

" ' Three hundred.'

" ' Three hundred guineas for this magnificent thoroughbred ' —' and fifty.'

" Eventually The Scout was ' bought in ' by Tatham for 450 guineas.

" ' We can well afford it,' he said, ' looking at it only from the mercenary point of view. I was prepared to bid up to the extent of my winnings.'

" As his winnings amounted to considerably over fifty thousand dollars, I smiled. I do not doubt that he would be prepared to carry out his promise, but the picture he conjured up of a bidder who would run a selling plater to fifty thousand dollars was amusing enough.

" Just before the last race I had an opportunity of speaking with Plant.

" ' How did he go ? ' I asked.

" ' I don't quite know how to describe it,' said the little man. ' He got away from the tape as if he'd been used to racing all his life. He was going like a fire engine, but I held him back to the leaders. Into the straight, Maher on the favourite looked round, and I knew Danny wasn't going too comfortably. Soon after that he took up his whip and then I sent The Scout after him. Go! It was like putting a motor car on its top speed! We went past Maher like—like——' He was at a loss for a simile. Then he asked—

" ' Where did you dig him up ? '

" I was unable to satisfy his curiosity. Other people I knew were asking the same question, and when a fortnight later we brought out The Scout to run in the Metropolitan Plate at Alexandra Park, the appearance of Tatham's commission installed it a hot favourite.

" By this time, however, Tatham had got into communication with several of the big starting price commissioners, and one of these, a man of unimpeachable integrity, had arranged to work all the S.P. Commissions.

" To those people who are unacquainted with the routine of the turf, I must explain that scattered throughout England, Scotland, and Ireland are thousands of commission agents who are prepared to open an account with any sportsman who can produce a banker's reference. Through these, bets may be made and settled weekly.

" Generally there is a time limit, and a restriction placed upon the size of the bet to be made. Thus, some agents will not accept a bet exceeding ten dollars, unless it is telegraphed a quarter of an hour before the advertised time of the race, or one of twenty-five dollars unless it is wired away thirty minutes before the race. By opening accounts with a number of these agents, it is possible to lay quite a respectable sum of money on a horse, even up to the very last moment. Our agent took the tedious work of organization off our hands, although Tatham would have dearly loved to carry the matter through himself.

" The story of the Alexandra Park race requires little telling ; it lacked any of the exciting features of the Windsor event. Plant again had the mount, and the start was effected from the gate opposite the stands. The Scout struck off ahead of the rest, but before the field had disappeared round the soup-plate course, Plant had pulled him back to fourth place. When the field came round the course for the second time he still held the same position. Coming into the home stretch, Plant brought him up neck and neck with the leader, and at the distance shot him out clear, winning in a canter by two lengths.

" After that The Scout missed his Kempton engagement.

" He had been entered for the Portland Handicap at Doncaster, and as a preliminary to this was brought out for a five-furlong dash at Lingfield. The opposition was poor, but they were approved sprinters, whilst The Scout had distinguished himself over a distance. In consequence (and because Tatham invested his money away from the course through S.P. offices), he started at the remunerative price of 100 to 8, and won easily by a neck.

"'We will keep him now for Doncaster,' said Holton. 'You would imagine that after what the public have seen, he would be a raging favourite for the Portland Handicap. But they will argue that he "beat nothing," that he was only a moderate horse in a bad field—I sincerely hope that the handicappers will take the same charitable view.'

"But the handicappers had a higher appreciation of The Scout's capabilities, and when the weights were published we found he had been awarded the 'steadier' of 122 lbs., an official estimate which was derided in more quarters than one.

"Tatham was not waiting for the end of the racing season before he made his purchases. The milling machinery was already ordered, the portable dwellings were under construction, and with our Lingfield winnings, he purchased two 4-in. quick-firing guns, which had been made to the order of a South American Republic, and left on the maker's hands.

"He also made extensive purchases of hoisting tackle, including a pair of fifty feet sheerlegs, and a winding engine. These were ready for delivery at once, and Hackitt took the ship round to Newcastle to receive them.

"The greater our success, the more ambitious grew Tatham's plans, and he now submitted a new scheme. It was to this effect. The *Scoutina* was to sail in August for the island, carrying the sheerlegs and hoisting gear, provisions and coal. A crew should be engaged to work her out.

"In October Tatham would charter a vessel to follow with the remainder of the equipment, including the guns, and a further stock of coal. (This was afterwards modified and a collier chartered to deliver at Tatham Island.) On the arrival of the chartered steamer, the crew and the officers of the *Scoutina* were to be transferred to her, paid off, and sent home.

"'Later,' said Tatham, 'we will buy a swift despatch boat to carry our gold to Rio, but my motto is, and always shall be, *festina lente*.'

"An astonishing claim.

"I have no exact knowledge of Tatham's winnings in the three races I have referred to. I know that he won more than fifty thousand at Windsor and over fifteen thousand at Alexandra Park, but as to Lingfield I am in the dark, but I have every reason to believe that it was an enormous sum. The *Sportsman*, in commenting on the race, said—

" ' Although The Fighting Scout started at an outside price, there is little doubt that he was the medium of a big gamble, for scarcely had the jockey weighed in, than telegrams conveying covering money flowed into the ring from every part of the country, and one prominent penciller alone received (fortunately for him too late) instructions to cover to the extent of $3000.'

" What makes me think that the Lingfield coup was of such importance was the alteration that came to Tatham's plans immediately afterwards. He gave up his humble lodgings and established himself in a palatial suite at the Cecil, and what is more significant his men followed suit, and accepted the change without apparent misgiving. He told me, too, that it was now costing the party $1000 a week to live, which meant that Tatham considered that he could afford an expenditure of $10,000 on purely personal comforts.

" It was just like him, that he ordered two sheets for The Fighting Scout, one to be worn at exercise and the other for paddock display. The paddock sheet was of woven silk with an embroidered border of gold, worked in a Byzantine pattern, and must have cost the greater part of two hundred dollars. There was a third sheet of green and silver—but this I persuaded him to keep hidden.

" ' It is the only way I can show my gratitude here,' he said. ' When I get back to my island I will have a stable built of white marble, with a gilded dome, and the interior shall be inlaid with slabs of *lapis lazuli*. Over the door I will place the inscription in letters of gold—

Amicus humani generis,

and on Sunday afternoons my people shall bring him offerings of flowers and corn.'

" His plans for this ideal city had not suffered through neglect. Going down to Lingfield, he had expatiated upon the novel feature of this creation of his. There were to be huge baths, a stadium, a State gymnasium, and the Perfect Church. This latter he spoke of with great earnestness.

" ' The church must not be a duty ; it must be a pleasure. To be looked forward to with as much eagerness as we look forward to a visit to a popular entertainment. There must be no hard pews and chilling architecture. I would have my people worship God as though God were a very desirable everyday acquaintance, and not a rich relation for whom we put on company manners, and of whom we stand in awe, lest He cut us out of His will.'

" He dealt with the subject in a spirit of reverence, but some of his illustrations were, to say the least, quaint.

" ' There shall be easy-chairs for the congregation to sit in, and footstools for the women. Men who want to smoke shall have a special gallery to themselves, and if in the course of the sermon anybody finds himself in need of refreshment, he shall have it. There will be little electric bells to summon the attendants. The minister must talk in an ordinary tone of voice, and not in a church voice, and abstract theology will be barred.

" ' We will have an organ to play the hymns, and those who want to sing shall sing, and those who don't can sit still and listen.'

" According to Tatham no service should last longer than half an hour, but, as he naïvely put it, for extra bad people a number of prayer-cells would be built where they could retire and pray in decent seclusion.

" I have often wondered since, exactly what Tatham would have made of his island, and his wonderful little community, had he been allowed to work his will. I do not doubt that he would have made a state unique in the world's history ; that without the outside help and guidance which he was destined to receive, he would have achieved a remarkable result.

" It might well have been a brilliant and bewildering triumph for his versatility and genius ; on the other hand, it might have been—because of the very greatness of his qualities—a tragic and disastrous failure. I cannot believe that it would have been so, but I say it very easily might have been. Idle it is to speculate upon the probable results of this or that happening, because as Tatham planned and schemed and elaborated to an end, Fate was surely but slowly leading him in a direction he did not wot of, shaping a course for him of which he did not dream.

" A week after the Lingfield race we met Eve Smith."

VIII

So far the history of Tatham Island had produced no woman, a remarkable circumstance. I find Mr. Callus more than usually interesting
in his descriptive work, and I have to thank him for having in this section
and hereafter reduced his recollection of the events to writing—an inestimable advantage, remembering that here we have a workman handling
familiar tools and insensibly conveying those right shades of expression
which the bald narrative of the stenographer is so apt to miss. From
hereon I have omitted the inverted commas which mark the fact that Mr.
Callus is describing the events depicted. His narrative is too interesting
for me to run the risk of confusing the reader by typographical pedantry.

I HOPE I have made it clear to you the kind of man Tatham
was and is.

If I have conveyed any other impression to your mind than
that he was high-minded, chivalrous, brave and resourceful, I
have failed in my description of the man.

Yet another characteristic was his encyclopædic knowledge
on subjects, some of them remarkably recondite. I pass over
his grasp of subjects such as gold and its chemistry, of mining
and such sciences as geology.

I go to the other extreme, and dismiss his conversance with
the intricacies of horse-racing. For instance, he was a store-
house of knowledge on prehistoric life, and I well remember
one night, on the ship, he drew me so vivid a picture of the
Megatherium that I could scarcely sleep that night. In some
respects he was almost childlike in his simplicity. He could be
outspoken on the most delicate subjects, and I am able to deal
fully, and, I believe, very accurately, with the incident of Eve
Smith for this reason.

I know that it is Tatham's wish that all that can be told about
the matter which you are investigating should be told.

I personally should not have reduced the story to writing but
for your inquiry. The history of Tatham Island is less a newspaper story to me than the subject of a memoir.

It was a Saturday night. We had spent the morning at the
Cecil in drawing up a scheme of fortification for the island.
Tatham's dream was a six-gun battery on Nicholas Point, commanding the submarine mouth of the river. He projected a
further battery on Cape Sydney, one commanding Kipling Cove,
and another in the Fallier Alps, west of Callus Heights. For the

present he said he would content himself with a gun at each end of the island, one on the unnamed eastern point, and the other at Nicholas Point. These two would practically command all sides of the island, and every approach.

After lunch we strolled into the Strand, and spent an afternoon at a matinée. We dined at 7 p.m., and after dinner Tatham expressed a desire to walk in the park.

It is difficult for me to remember at this moment by what progression of circumstances we came to secure our first introduction to the domestic life of the Smiths.

It may have been, and probably was so, that it was owing to the temporary and interesting friendships which Tatham was contracting at that moment with agents and manufacturers, that Mrs. Smith came into our zone. I have an idea that Tatham must have met her at one of those manufacturing demonstrations, where two or three score of bored visitors are conducted through a mile-long workshop, one of the directors explaining glibly, but quite unintelligibly, the function of each separate piece of machinery—a perambulation which usually ends in a tea given in the director's room.

Here it was in all probability that Tatham met the mild Mrs. Smith. Be that as it may, we had not gone far in the direction of the park before he stopped in consternation and looked at me severely.

" Callus," he said, " one of the duties which civilization imposes upon its products is the obligation, under which we all rest, to observe the social amenities."

After which preamble he deigned to explain that he had accepted an invitation for himself and for me too, to what he termed a " party."

I had visions of being called upon to sing, or do parlour tricks, and I hastily excused myself.

" You must come," said Tatham gravely. " I did perhaps, overstep the conventions, when, without consulting you, I accepted the invitation on your behalf. But I think you will enjoy yourself. Mrs. Smith is a lady of singular charm of manner, and has the gift, which so few women, and indeed, so few men, possess, of appreciating scientific endeavour at its true value."

From which I gathered that the lady had been engaged in impressing upon Tatham what a fine fellow he was.

I hesitated. I knew I should be bored stiff, but, I must confess, I was possessed by a curiosity to know exactly how Tatham would behave in that nebulous sphere which is called " society."

Mrs. Smith had a little house in Bayswater. It was in one of those long roads which connect Bayswater with Mayfair and where, at the Mayfair end, the houses grow narrower and narrower, crowding against one another as if in a panic, lest they stray into the more unfashionable portion of the street.

She was a woman, as I subsequently discovered, who had a passion for parties, and was never quite so happy as when she was making two guests groan where one had groaned before.

Since her entertaining area was severely restricted, it is not to be wondered that her little social plot was somewhat overcrowded.

Habitués of Mrs. Smith's " at homes " and functions were sufficiently well acquainted with the lay of the house to tuck themselves into odd corners and alcoves, but both Tatham and I found ourselves a little cramped for room in the tiny hall where six men were endeavouring to find pegs for their coats at one and the same time.

The drawing-room was on the first floor, and although the stairs leading up to it were somewhat narrow, Mrs. Smith carried out the illusion of a Foreign Office reception by receiving her guests on the first landing with her back to the bathroom door, and handing them over as they squeezed past, to an ill-fitted butler, who conducted them the three or four paces which separated end of stair from beginning of drawing-room.

She boasted that she never forgot names, and was wont to cite herself and King Edward as twin souls in this respect.

Indeed, from time to time, she found many startling phases of resemblance between herself and various members of the Royal Family.

The tiny drawing-room was uncomfortably crowded.

I found myself wondering, as I pushed my way through the press, by what extraordinary manœuvre Mrs. Smith held and attracted such a large and representative body of good-looking young men.

One had a lurking suspicion that as fast as they entered the drawing-room by the door, they surreptitiously escaped through the window.

There was that air of unreality which is frequently to be found in the small drawing-rooms of people bitten by the social bug.

" She called me Mr. Tinker," said Tatham's voice in my ear.

His voice almost trembled with chagrin. I tried to appease him.

" She called me Phillips," I responded, " though that is not my name, so far as I know. You must allow for lapses in the memory of a hostess who probably entertains thousands of people a year."

Tatham was silent, but I could see by a glance at his face that he was very annoyed indeed.

The press was thickest at one end of the drawing-room, and

to this we made, following the instinct which invariably draws man to man, for men like men in crowds.

"What is the attraction?" grumbled Tatham. "Is it not lamentable," he went on, without waiting for a reply, which as a matter of fact I was not prepared to offer, "that with all the joyous and bountiful gifts which nature has prepared and laid open for her children, men should be found who prefer the hot and fetid atmosphere of a drawing-room and the stimulations of artificial gaiety to that ante-chamber of heaven, the field? Does not the pettiness, the inconclusiveness of it, strike you? Think of the futility of effort——"

He got so far, and was warming to his subject, when the little crowd which stood between us and the attraction thinned, as a seafret thins before a westerly wind, and we saw, for the first time in our lives, Eve Smith.

She was standing near the fireplace listening to a short youth by her side, with some evidence of boredom.

I find it difficult, being unused to the description of women, to crystallize my first impression.

There have been many times when I have written with some fluency a word picture of Eve Smith, as she appeared to me. In another mood I have read it, and have seen how absolutely erroneous was my conception of her.

She was elusive, though sufficiently definite in her line and colouring. Her face was pale, and it did not strike me as being that perfect oval which the poet and painter demand.

My impression was that of a heart-shaped face, if you can imagine a heart which is a trifle narrower than that which adorns the letters and literature of the love-sick.

Her eyes were a rich dark blue. They were tremendously alive. Her mouth was generously large, but not noticeably so. Her lips were exquisitely shaped, her eyebrows pencilled delicately, with that little inquiring arch to them which your connoisseur of beauty finds so adorable.

Her hair, perfectly coiffured, was a mass of golden brown. About this she wore a little bandeau of dull gold.

Of these first impressions which I sometimes write, one is insistent. It is of a crowned queen; so proud and straight she stood, with a little tilt to her chin and the merest hint of condescension in her eyes, as she talked to the voluble youth who hung upon her words.

Her gown, cut low at the neck, was very plain. It was, if I remember, of black velvet, close fitting.

Her arms, bare to the elbow, were white and beautifully shaped; her hands—larger than one expected, but pretty. She had a plain gold bangle about her wrist, the only jewel she wore.

" Possibly a keep-sake," I thought, and then it occurred to me, and I afterwards justified the thought, that the Smiths were tolerably poor, and that Mrs. Smith's passion for the social game absorbed their slender income to the last farthing.

I looked at Tatham. He was staring at her—his lips parted, his eyes wide open, his head a little forward.

At any other moment he would have amused me ; but I had seen that look before, that strange earnestness and intensity with which he confronted the problems of life.

I was afraid that people might notice him and think him a boor. I had grown absurdly jealous for the reputation of Tatham, and I nudged him sharply. I might as well have dropped confetti on his greatcoat.

He continued to look, and the girl must subconsciously have become aware of the unwinking gaze fixed upon her, for she turned her head and faced him.

For a moment they stood thus, looking one at the other, then I saw a delicate pink creep into her face, and I caught Tatham's arm.

" Go and introduce yourself," I muttered, " and apologize for your rudeness."

Obeying rather the dictation of his inner self than any suggestion of mine, he went towards her, his hand outstretched.

" I am Captain Ta——" he began.

I was quick to rescue him.

" You know Mr. Deane, Miss Smith ? " I asked.

I did not know then that she was Miss Smith ; she might have been a niece for all I knew, but I had to take the bull by the horns and get him out of his difficulty. He was prepared to admit that he was the notorious Captain Tatham, and this before half a dozen interested people who were watching the scene curiously.

She must have taken it for granted that I knew her sufficiently well to act as Master of Ceremonies. She afterwards told me that she mistook me for a man named Wilcox—a wholesale jeweller, who was tolerated at Mrs. Smith's affairs because he had, on occasion, supplied souvenirs for exalted visitors.

She held out her hand, frankly, freely, to Tatham, and he took it. He held it, it seemed to me, an unconscionable time, but then I was a little overwrought. The responsibility of piloting Tatham through the social maze was getting on my nerves.

" I have heard about you, Mr. Deane," she said with a dazzling smile, which showed two rows of pearly teeth. " We do not often entertain such distinguished people."

She said this with a gentle note of mockery; but, as usual, Tatham took her very seriously.

"You must not think of regarding me as distinguished," he said gravely. "I hope, Miss Smith, that you and I shall be great friends. I will have no artificial barriers erected which may separate to any extent two people anxious to grow in acquaintance."

The girl looked puzzled. She had uttered the first conventional pleasantry which had come into her head. I am sure she never regarded Tatham as distinguished, even as important.

She remembered him as one about whom her mother had spoken in her practical and speculative way.

Mrs. Smith was engaged in the eternal quest for the missing segment. It was only a tiny segment that was required to make both ends of her circle meet. She speculated modestly on the Stock Exchange, and dreamt dreams of meeting a magnificent kindly man, who would give her the "tip" of her life.

Then she would buy shares. The market would undergo some extraordinary evolution, and the shares she bought at five dollars, less fortunate people would want to buy at six; then she would sell, and she would be exactly one dollar, per share, to the good.

And if she had had five thousand shares, why then she would have five thousand dollars!

It was very simple.

On such day-dreams as these, men grew rich; but they are usually the men who sell the shares to the dreamers.

Mrs. Smith had talked briefly to her daughter about the advice of a nice Mr. Deane. The girl had remembered that much of the conversation. Any person who could advise her masterful mother of the difficult arts of finance was qualified for the prefix "distinguished."

Do not misjudge me or her. I have never known her to be anything but sincere. On certain points, however, she adopted her mother's view rather than any of her own.

Existence was too short to bother, overmuch, about people who stood in the third row of life.

Fortunately Tatham neither knew nor guessed this. He accepted kindly estimates of himself literally and unquestioningly.

But the girl was undoubtedly puzzled. She could not understand whether Tatham was serious, or whether it was a form of humour which had just about then become popular, owing to the success of a certain socialist dramatist, with whose name I will not sully these fair pages.

"I am sure I shall be delighted," she murmured pleasantly.

She altered her position, tapping her foot nervously, an infallible sign that she was embarrassed. She looked from Tatham to the dark young man at her side.

He was of that build which is inelegantly called "stumpy." He was at once brown and ruddy. It was as though a thin mahogany stain had been superimposed upon the red cheeks of plump childhood. His eyes were jet black, and he was inclined to stoutness.

From which sketchy description you may gather that he was not particularly prepossessing.

He made up for homeliness of face in magnificence of attire. His dress suit was cut so well that he seemed, like another famous character, to have been melted and poured into it.

In the breast of his shirt blazed a diamond almost as big as a hickory nut. His links, when he raised his hand to caress his tiny moustache, radiated light. His bejewelled fingers reminded one irresistibly of the illuminations at Luna Park.

" Do you know Mr. de Costa ? " asked the girl.

Tatham bowed to the young man, and the young man bowed to him.

For some reason she did not introduce me. But, as I said before, she probably had the impression that she had already met me, and that I possibly knew her *vis-à-vis*.

" I think I have met you before, Mr. Deane," said the young man.

" I do not think we have met you," said Tatham, with deliberation.

" In our office ? " suggested Mr. de Costa, an encouraging smile on his thick lips.

" We have never been into your office," said Tatham.

" I'm perfectly sure I have seen you there," persisted the other.

He spoke English without any trace of foreign accent, but Xavier de Costa was as purely Brazilian as a Brazilian can be.

If he expected that Tatham would be satisfied with an exchange of platitudinous pleasantries with the girl, and then would withdraw, he was disappointed. If he imagined that he could draw Tatham into a discussion on so futile a question as his presence in an office at some remote period of his life, he was mad.

Tatham had a weightier interest. The thought that he might be *de trop* never occurred to him, and if I had suggested that his unconventional method of interesting others in his career and his aspirations was calculated rather to bore than to grip their imagination, he would have smiled, pityingly.

He diagnosed the girl's half-amused embarrassment as a natural nervousness in being suddenly confronted with a man of his attainments. He ignored the fact that he was not known as Tatham, that his accomplishments were associated with quite another, and by popular account, unpleasant, person in the girl's mind—if she had ever heard of them.

By some extraordinary mental convolution which was peculiarly Tathamesque, he credited her with a full appreciation of his genius, a lurking suspicion of his identity, and a comfortable ignorance of the illicit character of his adventures. Like the exigent little boy who demanded of the store-keeper two cents' worth of hundreds and thousands all pink — an infinitesimal candy, about the size of a pin's head variously coloured—Tatham wanted her to pick him out " all white."

" It is more than a pleasure to meet you, Miss Smith," he began in his oratorical manner. " There are some events in life, some landmarks which rise above the dreary path that meanders across the plain of eternity, which stand out——"

He orated on without drawing breath, so to speak. For his imagery he ransacked forest and field and plain ; the vegetable, mineral, and animal kingdoms contributed to the illustrations of his argument, and the girl stood, looking at him, wonderingly, a little frightened, a little—a very little—amused, a little—more than a little—bored.

As for Xavier de Costa he stood solidly by, taking no part in the conversation, twirling his moustache with a determined and injured air.

From sheer humanity I set myself the task of diverting Tatham's attention. I knew that my action was invested with that heroism which one reads about in books of travels, where a devoted servant sets himself the thankless task of attracting the attention of a tiger, feeding upon his fellow-creature, to his plump and trembling self. I succeeded, however, in giving the girl an opportunity for escape, but I drew down upon myself, as I had foreseen, all the heavy weapons in Tatham's arsenal. He was quite short with me. Yet, as I urged upon him, it was absolutely necessary for him to seek out Mrs. Smith and pay her that little attention which is due from a guest to his hostess.

Tatham seemed to have forgotten his earlier oration on the subject of social amenities ; at any rate, he was not inclined to listen to my suggestion, and his quite audible comments on my tactlessness disturbed me much less than they amused the audience which they created.

Fortunately Mrs. Smith came to my rescue. She was engaged in that process which is described in society columns as " mixing with her guests." In other words, she was making her slow way through the crowded little room, giving a nod here, a smile there ; some comment, generally misplaced, elsewhere. She left behind her a train of bachelors, who had, in acknowledging her tender inquiries after their wives, inferentially admitted such possessions.

She found Tatham, or Deane, as he was to the world, and from the manner in which she pounced upon him and led him forth, I gathered that the object of her search had been accomplished. She was a bird-like little woman, and reminded me irresistibly of some person I could not place. It was a long time before I realized that it was the Mrs. Leo Hunter who had so singularly impressed Mr. Pickwick. She was, I discovered, Eve Smith's stepmother, being the second wife of the gallant colonel who had long since passed over to the majority.

Mrs. Smith's poetical way of putting it was that he had taken his sword to heaven, but as to this I cannot speak with authority. I did not see Tatham again for the greater part of an hour. She had shown him an immense favour apparently, for she had carried him off for a private chat.

She was one of those women who have a den, half study, half boudoir, all roll-top desks and liberty knick-knacks. She prided herself upon being a thorough business woman (all this I gathered from Tatham), with a head for figures which meant periodical disputes between her and her broker, which induced piles of tragic correspondence between herself and her bank, and explained to a very large extent the domestic cataclysms which were of such frequent occurrence in her household.

To this den she led Tatham, and in the hour he spent with her he learnt as much of her private history, and much more of her financial standing than she knew herself.

He came back and rescued me at a period when I was bored to the point of tears. He was very important and very mysterious. He plunged into the crowd again to find Eve Smith. I think she saw him coming ; at any rate, I saw her look helplessly round, then face him with a scared look in her eyes.

Tatham was justifiably annoyed to find the little Brazilian still in attendance. I thought he would be, the moment I caught sight of the curly black head, and was immensely relieved when I got up to them to hear the girl visibly brighten and say—

" Must you really go, Mr. Deane ? "

Tatham said he really must go ; he said why he had to go, what he had to do ; the hours of anxious work which lay ahead of him, and he hinted of the destinies of people which would be affected by any longer abstention from their interest. He spoke of generations yet unborn whose fates were trembling in the balance; he laid down the well-worn thesis that social obligations should be subservient to stern economic realities.

If she thought she had seen the last of him after he had so unmistakably expressed his intention of retiring, she was deceived. She did not know Tatham. I always dreaded his perorations. She felt foolish and resented the cause. People at whom speeches are made in public invariably feel foolish; I know of no more infallible way of hurting the human vanity, supposing that Eve Smith had any such despicable quality, than that.

Yet, for all the exhaustive character of his farewell, Tatham remembered on his way home several things he had intended to say, and was half inclined to go back and say them. All the way to the hotel he could think of nothing else but her wonderful eyes, her refinement, her glorious voice, etc.

She was, he then told me, the daughter of an army officer who had died suddenly a few years before, leaving his second wife and his daughter the most meagre of incomes. This was the text on which he delivered an address, dealing with the duty of the state and the grudging gratitude of the nation. So far as I have since been able to trace, Eve's father was a colonel of infantry, who had spent some twenty years in various parts of the globe, missing active service the whole of his life, and finishing up with the command of a militia depot. Under these circumstances, Tatham's heroics about the " children of England's battle-scarred defenders " were beside the point.

Mrs. Smith, he said impressively, was " a wonderful woman, a splendid woman, a business woman."

" I can only hope," he said, " that Eve inherits her splendid qualities."

My protest that girls as a rule did not inherit the qualities of their stepmothers was passed unnoticed. When Tatham ordered his world to his own satisfaction he was not above adjusting the laws of progeniture. Mrs. Smith had sought his advice as to her investments. Tatham had fallen for it.

It is a subtle form of flattery employed by dowagers, who cannot hint at the physical attractions of their middle-aged and bald-headed admirers, and still retain their self-respect, but find in this oblique tribute to their business capacities an effective and profitable substitute.

But Tatham was not middle-aged, and the poison of the flattery had eaten deeper into his system.

" I am transferring five thousand shares in the Island's Hope Gold Mining Corporation," he said.

I gasped.

" The Island's Hope——? " I asked incredulously.

" The Island's Hope Gold Mining Corporation," said Tatham firmly.

" But you haven't got a company," I protested.

He looked at me a little sadly.

" It is one of the things I have overlooked," he said. " One of the essentials of our communal life. It did not, I confess, occur to me until that extraordinary woman was discussing such things as shares and bonds ; then I realised in a flash that it was impossible for me to help her because no such shares stood in my name. Have not," he asked impressively, " the great events of history which have transformed the world been born in a moment's inspiration ? Even as I sat there in the excellently appointed study—I must make a note, by the way, of the furnishing of that apartment ; I should like an office arranged on similar lines—the Island's Hope Gold Mining Corporation came into existence."

" In other words," I said with some asperity, " you created the mine in order to give her shares."

" I created the company," he said gravely ; " bountiful Nature, inscrutable Providence, the Alchemy of Time——"

I will not attempt to follow him through the maze of metallurgy in which he found himself. It lasted until we had reached the hotel ; it continued in the elevator ; he would have come into my room, and sat on the edge of my bed, to its conclusion, but I locked the door.

IX

THE EVIDENCE OF THE FOURTH WITNESS :
RICHARD CALLUS (*continued*)

It helps me considerably in my estimation of Captain Tatham's character to have the advantage of Mr. Callus's skilled powers of observation and record. Remembering the present association between the names of Tatham and Eve Smith, it is of vast importance that the growth of their acquaintanceship should be closely watched, and to my mind it has only been possible to gather the threads of the story by reason of the important part which a trained journalist took in the fashioning of the extraordinary history.

AN ordinary man would have waited a day or two before he attempted to renew acquaintanceship with a woman whose charms had created so profound an impression on him. But

Tatham was no ordinary man. He called the next day, and having no more idea of social conventions than a cow has of painting on silk, he chose a quarter to one in the afternoon.

Mercifully, both Mrs. Smith and her daughter were indulging in the luxury of a day's shopping, and Tatham came back to the hotel crestfallen and sat moodily at the lunch-table watching me eat. I expostulated with him.

"It was absurd to call at an hour like that," I said reproachfully.

"I thought they might ask me to lunch," said Tatham naïvely.

He refused to eat anything for a little while, and then his healthy appetite overcame his desire for starving to death, with the result that I had to wait another three-quarters of an hour at the table whilst he fed, which annoyed me intensely.

"Do you think if I called this afternoon——?" he asked.

"You'll make yourself a nuisance. Moreover," I said, as a bright idea struck me, "Mrs. Smith will not unnaturally regard your munificent gift of shares as an attempt to buy your right of entrance into the house at all inconvenient hours of the day and night."

His face fell, and he made no attempt to put his threat of calling into execution. Indeed, during the next few days he was so busy with his other work that I hoped his infatuation had died a natural death. I dreaded not so much the distraction of an engagement as the effect a blank refusal on the part of the girl would have upon his vanity. When, later, he mentioned the material prospects of the Smiths, I was sufficiently indiscreet as to suggest that they might well be left to work out their own salvation.

He turned on me and rended me in about twelve hundred well-chosen words.

"It is to such unsympathetic, pharisaical souls as yours," he said amongst other things, "that we owe the shocking and cynical disregard for infant life in England, the deterioration of the natural physique, the growth of anti-militarists in France."

I might have contested the point with him in spite of his inconsequence, but it was never worth while to meet Tatham in the dialectical field.

On the fourth day he called. I was secretly pleased to observe that he had taken my words to heart. At four o'clock in the afternoon he issued from his room, arrayed like a modern Solomon in all his glory. From the tips of his enamelled

American shoes to the crown of his glossy Bond Street hat he was the man about town. He did not take me with him.

He returned in an hour and a half considerably agitated.

"Come up to my room," he said shortly ; and wondering what on earth had happened, I accompanied him to the sitting-room which formed part of his suite. I waited for a few minutes whilst, as he described it, "he stripped those dam' things off," and when he came back in his lounge suit I saw that his face was a little white.

Now, when Tatham goes white, he is very angry indeed. My heart went down in my shoes because I thought I knew there was only one thing which could so disturb his equanimity, and that was that he had proposed to Eve Smith and had been rejected.

Such I found was the case, though he did not tell me so at the moment. Rather he directed the vials of his wrath upon two gentlemen who had had the singular bad taste to be present, and to monopolize much of the lady's time, during Tatham's visit.

Tatham would have sent them out, but they had apparently called to take the girl to a " five o'clock."

"It was impossible to say what I wanted to say," he said moodily, striding up and down the apartment, "so I hit upon a ruse."

He shrugged his shoulders.

"What was the ruse ? " I asked curiously ; but he seemed disinclined to go on.

"In love as in war," he began at last, "all means are justified. Remembering the seriousness of the issue, remembering the tremendous effect which the decision one way or the other might produce upon posterity, and remembering, too, that, in love as in war, as I say, we come against the elementary passions which are superior to the trivial conventions of modern life——"

I waited, wonderingly.

"My suggestion to the two young men, one, as I have told you, was De Costa, and the other a Mr. William Dixon, of 43 Claremont Gardens, S.W.," he added, imposingly and significantly, "my suggestion was, I contend, perfectly pardonable and quite admissible within the rules of war. It was that I had a friend who in a moment of exuberation had struck a policeman."

I gasped.

"As a result of that unlawful act my friend had been arrested and taken to Bow Street police station. I myself was a stranger in the country ; I had not sufficient influence to secure his release. Would those gentlemen of their charity drive to Bow Street and vouch for the respectability of my unfortunate friend."

He said all this hesitatingly yet hurriedly : there were long pauses between each sentence. Tatham was obviously ill at ease.

"And who," I asked slowly, "might this unfortunate friend of yours be?"

Tatham looked at the ceiling thoughtfully.

"If by any chance," he said, "I have overstepped——"

"Not me!" I cried in horror. "You didn't say it was me?"

Tatham nodded silently.

"I will only say this in extenuation," he said, with that seriousness which made all his actions so real and plausible, "that I took particular care to impress upon them that you were perfectly sober."

I fell back in the chair helplessly.

What could one do, what could one say, with a man like this?

"Well," I asked at last, having resigned myself to the loss of what little character I possessed, "what did these two young people do?"

"I must confess," said Tatham, "that they were very decent. They went at once, took a taxi-cab and drove straight away to the police station. Not finding you there, and ascertaining by telephone that you were not at Upper Mayfair Street, they came back. In the meantime I had thrown myself upon the mercy of Eve."

"Did you call her Eve?" I asked.

"I called her Eve," said Tatham gravely, "because that is her name. I put before her as much of my prospects as I deemed it expedient to reveal. I gave her a brief *résumé* of my views on love and matrimony and the duty which we owe to the future. I told her in the terms which I have discovered are usual" (I afterwards found that Tatham had sent out a comprehensive commission to the nearest bookstall, for all the latest novels in which the love interest dominated), "that I loved her and would endeavour by a life-long service, by a devotion which would be unique in the history of the world, to make her life an increasing joy and pleasure."

He was walking up and down all the time he spoke. He stopped in front of the window and stared out ; thunder clouds were banking up over South London and on the murky horizon there was the flicker of lightning.

"That is as it should be," he said.

Tatham was approving of the elements ; it was not the first time he had suggested that the incidence of natural phenomena were directed by an all-wise Providence to coincide with his moods.

" She could not agree," he said. " She was startled, I thought at first she was angry ; but possibly I am doing her an injustice."

" What of the young men ? "

" They returned as I was going," said Tatham.

He swung round on me.

" I have their cards and their addresses—that is what I wish to see you about. You will call on them to-morrow and arrange a meeting."

I had no words. I simply arose from my chair with my mouth open.

" Arrange a meeting ! " I stammered.

" Arrange a meeting," said Tatham. " They used language to me which I will not permit any man to use. Moreover, what they said was in the presence of my future wife."

" But she refused you ! "

" My future wife," repeated Tatham, in such a tone of decision as left no room for argument.

" But what do you mean by a meeting—you don't for one moment imagine that these people will fight a duel ? "

" That remains to be seen," said Tatham. " I think that Hyde Park in the early hours of the morning would be an admirable rendezvous. You may leave to them the choice of weapons. I know very little about these fancy small swords which duellists favour, but if they will be kind enough to choose cavalry swords, I should be glad. I will fight them with knives, or of course with rapiers, if they prefer those weapons. I have no doubt that I shall make myself proficient in a few hours. As honourable men, they will not of course desire to take me at a disadvantage——"

He discussed the punctilio of duelling at some length. There was no use in arguing with him. I had of course to see these people to explain in justice to myself, although I should not have done so had Tatham objected.

I made my calls the next morning, feeling that I was half as much a lunatic as Tatham, but banking rather upon my knowledge of human nature and the certainty that neither of these two young products of the twentieth century would for one moment countenance Tatham's preposterous suggestion.

I called upon Mr. Dixon first. He was a bright, pleasant-faced youth, with a keen sense of humour, I am happy to say, and when I put Tatham's suggestion forward he burst into a roar of laughter.

" I'll go round and see old Deane myself," he said. " I was rather rude, I admit, but one doesn't like to have one's leg pulled in front of a girl. I'll make it all right with him. You go along and see the nigger."

From which I gathered that there was no love lost between him and young De Costa.

" What a beggar your man is ! " Dixon went on admiringly ; " swords and pistols in Hyde park—it's a perfectly ripping idea. When can I find him at home ? I'll go round and give him all the apology he wants."

I left him, calling down blessings upon his sensible, well-brushed head.

De Costa had a flat in Jermyn Street. He was dressing when I was announced, and kept me waiting some time, which did not add to my love for him. He greeted me surlily when he came eventually. In a few words I explained the unconscious part I had played in the business. He accepted my explanation with an ungracious grunt. Then I came to the serious business of the interview.

" Mr. Deane has sent me," I said, " as a result of a certain act of discourtesy which you showed to him yesterday."

I thought I detected a look of alarm in his face.

" Mr. Deane considers that that discourtesy was absolutely unwarranted, and has asked me to demand from you the satisfaction which one gentleman is usually prepared to give to another. As the challenged party," I went on carefully, " you will naturally have the choice of weapons."

His face went a pale green and his mouth and eyes opened to their fullest extent.

" What ? " he stammered, " is he challenging me to a duel ? "

I gave a little bow.

" If you can name a friend I can complete the arrangements without bothering you."

" But—but ! " he said, " duelling isn't allowed ; it's against the law ! You've no right to challenge me to a duel in England. I shall go to the police. I think it's a disgraceful thing. You'll get yourself into serious trouble ! " he went on incoherently. " You know, I've studied law—and I feel it is my duty to warn you. It's monstrous ! I will not fight Mr. Deane. If he thinks there is any apology due to him——"

" He does think so," I said.

"Suppose I did apologize," the young Brazilian asked, " would that be an end to the business ? "

I nodded again. A look of relief came to his face ; he was shaking like a man with ague.

" I've never had a thing like this happen to me before," he said almost pathetically. " I'm sure if I went to the police there would be awful trouble about it. It is only because I do not wish to bring in the name of a lady who was present, and who I hope "—he made a feeble attempt to smile—" will one day stand in closer relation to myself than she does at present, that I allow this matter to pass over. You may tell Mr. Deane that I will write."

I went back to the hotel whistling, and found Tatham and Dixon already lifelong friends. They were discussing a large bottle of Perrier Jouet in Tatham's sitting-room, and the young man was jovial, not to say hilarious.

I think I arrived in time to prevent Tatham, in a burst of confidence engendered by the other's geniality, from confiding all his plans to him. Tatham had arranged for Mrs. Smith to come to tea at the hotel that afternoon ; he was not without hope that she would bring Eve with her, but in this he was disappointed. Mrs. Smith said that her daughter had a headache.

The tea was not a pleasant function ; most of the entertaining devolved upon me. Tatham was silent and taciturn. He had one of the worst humps I ever remember his developing. Mrs. Smith was obviously anxious to discuss the question of these shares which Tatham in mistaken generosity had promised her.

To my surprise he produced from his inside pocket a share certificate of conventional shape and design and handed it across to her. I had time to notice that it was almost wet from the printer ; that it was numbered in accordance with the company laws of England, and that it bore the flourishing inscription : "Island's Hope Gold Mining Corporation."

The lady was most voluble in her thanks, and, like a lady, not satisfied with being possessed with this outward and visible sign of her share in the enterprise, she began a series of cross-examinations, with the object of extracting from Tatham or myself the immediate prospects of the investment.

She caught me at a disadvantage, but not so Tatham, for he had the whole of the corporation organized. He told her the extent of the mine, the amount of ore in sight, talked learnedly of the difficulties of haulage, water power, and stampage. That mine, though but a patch of earth, without so much as a borehole to testify to its genuineness, was a real tangible thing to Tatham. He saw its slender smoke stacks, the tracery of its headgear against the western sky ; he heard in imagination the roar of the stamp mills and watched the dump heaps growing day by day.

I think Mrs. Smith left us with the pleasing impression that if the mine wasn't working at exactly that moment, it was only because Tatham was not near by to direct operations.

X

THE EVIDENCE OF THE FOURTH WITNESS :
RICHARD CALLUS (*continued*)

I could have wished to include in this history a statement by Don Alphonzo De Costa, but neither he nor his son was prepared to give me the information I sought. I have received from the attorney of Mr. De Costa, senior, a communication to the effect that any reference to his firm would be met by a writ for libel ; but I am advised that under the terms of the Act of Congress dealing with official publications, my statements are privileged.

ALL the time Tatham was going ahead with his work. There were innumerable conferences to which the men were invited. Unfortunately August and September were two busy months with me. I was in the South of Spain five days before the Portland Plate was run, but I managed to clear up the story I was on and catch the northward express. In Madrid I received a wire from Tatham, an imploring wire that asked me to hurry home. It informed me that The Fighting Scout would be started for the race at Doncaster. The next afternoon I reached Paris, and the following afternoon I was in London.

I found Tatham a little finer drawn than I expected to see him. I had anticipated that the luxury of the life he was enjoying might make him a little disinclined to face the inevitable hardships which awaited him on Tatham Island. But he was all eagerness to get back. He told me that he had seen Eve Smith several times, and that she had given him a very solemn talking to and had agreed to forget the past.

He had apparently again fallen foul of young De Costa, " whose unwarrantable aspirations " (I quote Tatham's own words) had aroused the bitterest antagonism which the bosom of my friend was capable of harbouring.

We spent the evening talking of the work and discussing the prospects of The Fighting Scout. At eleven o'clock that night I arose to go to my room, for I was tired ; I had had a long and particularly trying journey and was looking forward to bed with some enjoyment, when a waiter came in with a card. He handed it to me, and I glanced at the pasteboard with some surprise. It was inscribed—

" Mr. Xavier De Costa
and
Mr. Alphonzo De Costa."

The latter was written in pencil. I showed it to Tatham.

" I wonder what they want," I said ; "it's a weird hour to call."

Tatham's face brightened up.

" I wonder——" he began, but did not finish his sentence. It might have been that he imagined that visit would symbolize an act of self-abnegation of which I am certainly satisfied young De Costa was incapable.

All his doubts were disposed of a few minutes later when the sulky young Brazilian, looking stouter and more unpleasant than ever, came into the room and introduced his father.

The latter was no taller than his son, but was thin and of the wiry type. His face was lean and drawn, and clean shaven, save for a black moustache, plentifully shot with grey. His head was as bald as an egg, except for a little fringe of hair which circled the back of the scalp. He was darker than his son, and his English was not good. He bowed ceremoniously to us both.

" This is my father," said young De Costa.

Something made me look at Tatham. He had the faintest of smiles upon his lips as at some amusing recollection.

" You know my father, I think," said young De Costa.

" I haven't that pleasure," replied Tatham.

The older man favoured Tatham with a malicious little grin.

" I think we have done business together, Mr.—er——"

" Deane," said Tatham.

" Is it Deane ? " asked the other, innocently. " I seem to remember another name. May I sit down ? "

Tatham apologized for his rudeness. He pushed forward two chairs, and the men seated themselves. They were both in evening dress ; in De Costa senior's shirt front blazed a diamond even larger than that which his son affected on such occasions.

" I may recall to you, Mr.—Deane," there was an offensive little pause before the name, " that I am engaged in the shipping trade. I sometimes send cargoes to South America."

He smiled again.

" That is very interesting," said Tatham. " I think shipping is one of the most fascinating branches of commercial endeavour."

" I am glad you think so," said the old De Costa. " Sometimes," he continued, " I find it necessary to engage a supercargo, to carry out the more delicate and intricate negotiations which are sometimes associated with the transference of the goods shipped."

Tatham nodded.

" I quite understand the functions of the super-cargo," he said.

" Some years ago," the old man went on reminiscently, " I had to send rather an important cargo to one of the Islands of the West Pacific." He shrugged his shoulders and waved his hands in one motion. "I cannot recall exactly where the cargo was to land, or what it consisted of, but I have a most vivid recollection of a gentleman who called upon me at my office in Little Saville Street on one occasion. And I also remember having engaged him to carry out certain duties. In so engaging him it was necessary to take him into my confidence. To an extent——" He smiled. "For instance, I had to explain that he would pick up a collier at a certain point at sea and that he would land bales of hardware in a very difficult place."

"In the Philippines," said Tatham, cheerfully, "and it was not hardware, but rifles, if I remember rightly."

"As to that," the other hastened to say, "I have no distinct recollection. At any rate, there was an accident ; my coal was stolen ; my collier which I specially chartered to meet my ship was met by another. The coal was stolen, I repeat. Later, my ship was held up by a make-believe warship and the merchandise was removed, against the captain's wish. That, Mr.—er—Deane, was piracy."

"It was piracy," admitted Tatham, pleasantly, "a gross act of piracy, undoubtedly."

"I am glad you agree," said De Costa.

"What would you call the act of running guns for half-breed Philippinas ? " asked Tatham.

The old man flushed. It was not the accusation which annoyed him ; it was that horrid word "half-breed."

"That would not be piracy," said Tatham, drily, "that would be just an act contrary to every civilized law. Yes," he said, "I am Tatham. I don't hide it from you. I took your coal ; I took your rifles. The rifles you were sending to niggers to enable them to shoot down white men."

"Mr. Tatham ! " said the old man, jumping up and springing to his feet.

"The rifles you were sending to niggers, I repeat," said Tatham, "so that they might snipe the solitary pickets of the United States army — so that they may murder and terrorize the helpless and unarmed islanders. You're not a fool, you know the breed of the Puljanes. Why, you're one yourself."

It was curious to see the old man wilt under Tatham's vitriolic tongue. It was as though he insensibly did homage in that moment to the dominant race. Despite his vast riches, despite his undoubted influence, he was a native in the presence of a white man.

Under the spell of Tatham's mastery he cringed. Not so the son. He was one generation nearer whiteness. With a horrible noise, which was half a scream and half a strangled cry of hatred, he leapt at Tatham.

Tatham half turned. His hand went out rigidly. It seemed to me that the young Brazilian did not check in his flight but rather continued it, describing a curve about the spot where Tatham stood, until he pulled up with a crack against the opposite wall and went down in a heap.

I hate to see a grown man crying, yet that was the unpleasant spectacle which young De Costa afforded as he got up slowly to his feet.

They were tears of wrath and mortification, but they were none the less tears. He sobbed his anger, his impotence, wildly.

" I'll fix you, Tatham ! " he cried. " I'll be even with you for this. I'll have the police on your track ! "

" You can give them all the information you care to," said Tatham, calmly. " You may at the same time add an interesting chapter to your parent's biography."

The youngster was half mad with rage. He would have again essayed an attack, but the old man caught him round the waist and pulled him back.

It was the old man whom I feared. He was calm, but his eyes blazed terribly.

" You will hear again from me, Mr. Tatham."

" I trust not," said Tatham, as he opened the door for his visitors.

An ordinary man would have been satisfied to have allowed his visitors to depart in peace, but Tatham was no ordinary man. He followed them into the corridor and addressed them at length, raising his voice as they went farther and farther from him. He followed them along the passage to the elevator and delivered an address which, were it reproduced in pamphlet form, might fittingly be headed " Some Remarks on the Laws of Nations in Relation to Neutrality as Affecting Insurgents."

He came back to the room perfectly cheerful. The visit had acted like a tonic on him.

" We shall have to get moving now," he said. " Old man

De Costa is going to take very definite steps to bring about my undoing."

" But he dare not report this matter to the police," I said.

Tatham smiled.

" There are other ways," he said cryptically.

He was on his way to his room, but turned back.

" Do you think you could manage to snatch a few hours from your sleep to assist me ? " he said. " I am going into ways and means, and the question of the power station is bothering me."

Tired as I had been, I had also experienced something of the refreshment which excitement brings, and for three hours he and I were seated together, working away at that infernal power station.

It was ludicrously like a jigsaw puzzle into which one piece would never fit—or if it fitted some other essential portion must necessarily be left out. The obstinate piece in question was the power station. Try as we did we could not include it in the scheme on our present resources.

At last Tatham, with a sigh, admitted failure.

" I am afraid we shall have to let it go," he said, "unless " (here he spricked up) " unless we can get a good win at Doncaster."

I shook my head dubiously.

I do not like Doncaster as a gambling venue, although it is the heaviest betting meeting of the year, and most certainly I have never regarded the Portland Plate as an attractive medium for speculation.

He looked at his watch. It was half-past four.

" It is too late to go to bed," he said. " I will make some coffee."

He had had an electric kettle fixed in his room, and he was something of a cook. The coffee was delicious, and was greatly needed. He was sitting at the window watching the east sky grow grey and sipping his coffee meditatively, when he suddenly turned to me—

" Bath and shave," he said. " I've got a great idea."

I looked at him suspiciously. I do not like Tatham's great ideas—especially such great ideas as are likely to occur to him at half-past four in the morning. Nevertheless I felt the walk, which the preparation implied, would do us both good.

The church clocks were striking five when we turned into the deserted Strand. Save for a fruiterer's cart or two, which had strayed from Covent Garden, and were anchored in the middle of the Strand, there was little sign of life.

Tatham turned westward.

" If we can get a cab, so much the better," he said.

" You'll probably pick one up at Charing Cross," I said. " Is there any great hurry ? "

He nodded.

" There is a hurry," he admitted.

Under those circumstances it was probably fortunate that we found a waiting taxi.

I did not hear what directions Tatham gave to the man. I had an idea that the excursion had something to do with The Fighting Scout.

Tatham was quite capable of setting forth on a twenty-mile walk to Epsom, without any more substantial preparation than the coffee he had made. It was for this reason that I gladly welcomed the sight of the solitary taxi standing in the station courtyard.

As a matter of fact, we did not turn south, but pursued a way west and north.

" Where are we going ? " I asked suddenly.

" We're going to call on the Smiths," said Tatham.

I looked at him in amazement.

" Call on the Smiths ? " I said incredulously. " At this hour of the morning ? Are you mad ? "

He evidently was not mad—at least, he was under that impression.

The cab deposited us in the silent street, and we walked along till we came to the house. Tatham hesitated whether to knock or ring, and decided upon knocking.

He had knocked half a dozen times before the shuffling of slippered feet told us that our efforts had succeeded. A sleepy servant admitted us, albeit reluctantly. She asked us to stand in the hall, while she went to arouse her mistress.

" Remember," said Tatham, solemnly, " that it is only Miss Eve that we wish to see."

I would gladly have excused myself. I foresaw a very unpleasant experience ahead of me. At best I could only be present to witness Tatham's chagrin and disappointment. At the worst, I might be irretrievably damned in the eyes of all decent people, for not even the most charitable would imagine that I had accompanied my friend on a social call at five o'clock in the morning, whilst in possession of all my faculties.

The servant came down again in her wrapper and led us to the drawing-room.

Tatham with deplorable familiarity pulled the blinds up. He was perfectly cheerful—that is the remarkable circumstance. It seemed that he had no doubt whatever as to what would be the result of his visit.

In five minutes the girl came in. She wore a long kimono of

dark blue, edged with Russian embroidery, and she had hidden the glory of her hair under a boudoir cap.

She looked singularly beautiful. I could not have imagined any woman looking so pretty under such trying circumstances.

She was worried too. Naturally she could not fathom the meaning of this unexpected visit.

Afterwards I learned that the only solution that came to her mind was that the mine, in which her trusting mother held shares had proved an appalling failure, and that the call was justified by the urgency of the intelligence. At that time she did not know that her mother had put no money into the concern.

" I have called to see you, Miss Smith," said Tatham, gravely, " on a most important matter, and I know you will forgive me if I say what I have to say in the presence of my friend."

I was waiting for his next words with anxiety. I hadn't the slightest idea that Tatham even contemplated the extraordinary act which was in his mind.

" Last night, or rather in the early hours of this morning, I had an interview with Mr. De Costa," said Tatham.

He went on to give particulars of that interview. I watched her face all the time he was talking. There was a new light in it. Evidently Tatham had made good use of his time, and the curious friendship, begun against her will and in spite of the rebuffs which she had administered, had grown steadily in the right direction. But for this fact I doubt very much whether she would have even come down to see him.

She seemed more than ordinarily interested ; rather as though she were eager for all he could tell her. The light of sympathy was in her eyes. She sat on one of those hard, straight-backed chairs which are to be found in London drawing-rooms, and are designed to discourage lengthy visits, her hands clasping her crossed knees, as step by step, concealing nothing, exaggerating nothing, omitting nothing—except perhaps his own foresight and resourcefulness—Tatham took her from Cape Town *via* St. Paul de Loanda to Tatham Island and back again.

Now and again he referred to me for confirmation, but in the main his eyes did not leave her face. When he had finished there was a pause. Then she said, gently—

" I understand, Captain Tatham, and I appreciate your confidence. I am glad you have told me, because Mr. De Costa himself gave me a version last night which was not as complimentary to yourself as you have made it."

She smiled a little at the left-handed compliment she had passed.

" But why," she asked, " have you come ? "

" You are entitled to know that," said Tatham. " I must hurry forward all my arrangements and go back to the Island. I cannot go back till I know one thing. I cannot wait a day," he said vehemently, " with one doubt in my mind. Miss Smith——"

He leaned forward, his hands tightly clasped, his face tense and drawn, a new Tatham, a Tatham I had never seen before. The strong clean soul of the man shone in his face.

" I want a partner," he said, " I want—you ! "

He jerked out the last word. He made no declaration of love, and I should have sunk through the floor with shame if he had done so, but that she saw the dumb devotion in his eyes, I do not doubt.

Even I, who am no sentimentalist, could see it plain enough, and was sorry for Tatham.

She rose slowly and looked down at him, still in the same attitude in which he had made his plea, and a look of pity and something else came over her face.

" I am sorry, Captain Tatham," she said in a low voice, " I cannot agree, though I recognise how great an honour you have done me."

He got up ; he seemed to shake himself and drew a long breath.

" You cannot agree," he repeated.

She did not trust herself to speak. She shook her head slowly.

Then a pause, one of those seemingly interminable pauses so trying to the nerves. Neither of the two spoke. Tatham's eyes were on the floor ; hers, filled with pity, were on his face. It seemed that five minutes passed like this, though as a matter of fact the period was less than a minute.

Then Tatham said, " Oh ! "

That was all he said. It was not an " Oh " of pain, or an " Oh " of surprise, or an " Oh " of indifference. It was just " Oh ! "

XI

THE EVIDENCE OF THE FOURTH WITNESS :
RICHARD CALLUS (*continued*)

Again I testify to the extraordinary thoroughness with which Mr. Callus sets himself to secure material for this eleventh section—though in doing so he was unaware of the use to which his investigations would be put.

He tells me that he has based the section upon a very frank correspondence which he enjoyed with Eve Smith and upon the result of statements made to him by Martha Ann. I may here remark that when months after the events here described Martha Ann married a milkman, who subsequently embezzled his master's money, it was due to the influence of Mr. Callus that the charge was withdrawn and a new situation discovered for the erring man. Probably to the gratitude engendered by this intervention may be traced the completeness of Mr. Callus's knowledge of what transpired in 79 Upper Mayfair Street.

A JOURNALIST differs from all other writers in his overmastering passion for facts. I will forgive you if you smile at this statement, or if, being one of the " other writers," you are intensely indignant. Yet, being a journalist, I have few illusions. I know that scientific and learned writers who prepare long, elaborate, and tiresome papers for the edification of Royal Societies, more frequently square their theories with actualities than does the little-space man, who counts his income in lines.

I have known even great and highly placed travellers to describe their sojourn in foreign lands, their hunting experience and their privations, in language more graphic than accurate.

I have known, too, great Divines preaching before distinguished congregations, who have illustrated their arguments with stories of an entirely fictitious character—with stories, which so far from having any foundation in fact, were evolved in the preachers' studies on the night before their recital.

The journalist has the " find out " habit. He is not satisfied with the things he is told, and most certainly he is sceptical of the things he reads ; and, in the main, his hobby is to drag from their beds, in the early hours of the morning, important and irate citizens, to confirm or refute the scraps of intelligence, which the ordinary writer would take as read, and would adjust according to the requirements of his work.

All that I know about the Smiths' menage I have learnt by inquiry. The sense of diffidence, which ordinarily inspires a man to shun discussion of his neighbour's affairs with his neighbour's servants, is no longer part of my equipment.

That delicacy was killed at an early period of my career, by a ruthless and coarse city editor, who taught me that the word " Private " written across a door, or a career, was an invariable indication of some crooked business going on behind, which it was my duty to record for the benefit of a journal which, in those days, paid me twenty-five dollars per.

So that all I can tell of the Smith menage is entitled to bear the Hall Mark of authenticity. For what Eve had not told me herself, or what Mrs. Smith has not confided at various moments, has been supplied by an unconscious information bureau, presided over by the decayed butler of the household.

When we left the house that memorable morning, to return to the hotel after our fantastic and fruitless quest, Eve Smith sat for quite a long time in the little drawing-room.

It was an apartment which shone in the merciless grey light of the early morning. At such an hour, as I had observed, you saw the mark of the cleaner's vacuum brush, the discoloration where an amateur varnisher had endeavoured to renovate the chipped chairs, the thinness of the carpet here and there, and most appalling of all, the blatant artificiality of the " Gloire de Dijon " roses, which Mrs. Smith had brought back from Ostend with her the previous year.

Eve had taken a seat by the window and was sitting on it sideways, one arm thrown across the back and the other twisting and untwisting a piece of loose embroidery upon her kimono.

She was thankful at that moment that her mother was a heavy sleeper and had not been aroused by the summons.

Eve Smith hoped that she was a dutiful daughter. There were times when she came perilously near being glad that she was not. This was a moment when the presence of her mother would have sent her to her room.

It was good to be here alone, in the silence and the sweet light of the early day, to think this problem over— for Tatham had become a problem.

A month ago she would have dismissed his proposal with a laugh—and found relief in the sight of his disappearing back.

But now this tall brown man, with his obvious sincerity, his interminable speeches, his earnestness which verged upon pomposity, had taken a place with her.

He filled a niche no other man had occupied ; could occupy, to do Tatham justice, for Nature does not create duplicates of Tatham's quality.

Exactly where was that niche ? This speculation puzzled her. If she could answer that question after long deliberation and self-analysis, the problem was a problem no longer.

Where did he stand ? At that moment of time she had no feeling of love as young people understand love, no quickening of the pulse at his approach, no blotting out of her soul's sun at his departure, or unsatisfied voidance of soul at his continued absence.

Indeed, she had none of the conventional symptoms, and might be excused the belief that, so far as love was concerned, there was no bond between Tatham and herself.

And yet——

She walked to the French windows and, opening them, stepped out on to the little stone balcony. She looked up and down the street ; there was nobody in sight ; it would be little short of a social crime for any of the inhabitants of Upper Mayfair Street to be seen abroad at that hour save in evening dress.

Insensibly she found herself looking long, and a little wistfully, in the direction which she knew Tatham must have taken. She had a quick imagination, and a working knowledge of the neighbourhood, and I do not doubt that she pictured Tatham and his embarrassed friend, throughout the whole route, back to the hotel.

But Tatham was something more to her than a friend, though he was not even a friend in the accepted sense. The confidences, which mark the growth of friendship, had been all one-sided. It had been Tatham who had talked; be sure of that. She had listened excellently. Were I a cynic I should say that in that fact lay the foundation of Tatham's love.

But in this I should be unjust. Tatham's passion was an inspiration, a thing born of a momentary glance : love at first sight, though I hate the term.

To fulfil the requirements of the ideal, those two souls should have leapt together to light, as two chemical elements, dormant apart, will, on impact, forsake their independent properties and mingle riotously in the creation of a newer element.

But Tatham had done all the leaping, the girl had been but a passive agent, a screen to reflect his brilliancy. That is the simile I want : Tatham was a dazzling search-light that played on Eve Smith. She, herself, produced no increase in the power of illumination.

It was absurd to say that Eve Smith was cold. All women are cold—just as all men are liars. In a dark room a diamond is indistinguishable from half a brick. People who when groping in the gloom of ignorance in a vain search for the furnace which they felt must burn within the heart of Eve Smith, not infrequently came up against her refrigerating plant, and retired in disorder, composing wicked little epigrams.

She stood for a long time on the balcony, then returned to the room.

The servant, who had awakened her, still waited respectfully. Her name was Martha Ann, and she had in her colourless composition no romance that I have been able to trace. Her hour for rising was seven, and she had risen at five : that was all.

" Do you want me, miss ? " she asked with offensive patience.

Eve shook her head, and the girl went off.

" I don't suppose I shall get to sleep now," she said bitterly. " A nice time in the morning for gentlemen to call ! "

She said many other things, but was careful to wait until her voice was only represented to the girl below by a succession of incomprehensible sounds, the tenor of which might be grasped from the fact that each sentence ended on a high note.

I do not know whether Eve Smith went back to bed that memorable morning, but when Martha came down at the conventional hour she found her young mistress fully dressed, moreover dressed for the street.

" I am going to Covent Garden to buy some flowers, Martha," said Eve.

" What a house!" said Martha, and raised her eyes to the ceiling.

It was a glorious morning. The air was sweet and clean ; the flood of golden sunlight which bathed the green spaces of the city squares and made aureate avenues of the long orderly streets was a veritable elixir of life.

There was a spring even in the hard asphalt pavement that morning, and Eve Smith found herself singing quietly to herself as she walked along.

Covent Garden Market was a stone's throw from the hotel which housed Tatham. An hour later she was standing in the Strand, her arms filled with dewy blooms, looking with a thoughtful eye upon the great block of buildings which constituted the caravanserai.

I cannot tell you what passed in Eve Smith's mind, but I know that after standing there in meditation for a few minutes she turned and walked briskly towards Trafalgar Square, and made her way home by the shortest route.

Breakfast was seldom a pleasant meal in Upper Mayfair Street. The urbanity, the graciousness, and the Foreign Office manner of Mrs. Smith were never on view at so early an hour. The great hostess of 11 p.m. became the vinegary housekeeper of 9 a.m.

It was as though Nature had reversed her processes, and had evolved from the overnight butterfly a most business-like grub.

There was a pile of letters by the side of Mrs. Smith's plate when she came down to breakfast. Eve had already begun her meal, and the elder woman gave her a slight peck in the region between the eye and *superior maxilla* which signified the automatic continuance of her devotion.

She flounced into her chair, unfolded her napkin, glanced at her papers, and criticized the bacon, at one and the same time.

Eve regarded her idly. Instinctively she had closed all the soundproof doors of her mind on her stepmother's entrance.

" Bills," said Mrs. Smith, grimly. " We shall have to draw in our horns."

Eve had never completely satisfied herself as to what were

the horns to which Mrs. Smith invariably referred. If it was the cornucopian horn, it was generally drawn in empty.

" Here's this exasperating broker of mine," said Mrs. Smith, looking at a long Statement of Accounts. "I told him particularly not to sell Long Island Gas until it reached eighty-four, and here he has sold it at eighty-one ! "

" It is now seventy-six," said Eve, drily. " If you had waited for your eighty-four you might have lost much more money ! "

She had taken to a study of the Share Market and its report from sheer self-defence.

Mrs. Smith opened another letter. It was very short, and apparently unpleasant.

" Good God ! " said Mrs. Smith.

Her language at breakfast was generally violent. It was in a sense an act of devotion, since it had been acquired from her militant husband, who long since had carried his sword to heaven.

" What is the matter ? From the bank, I presume," said Eve.

Mrs. Smith invariably kept her most vivid expletives for the bank.

" He says I am eighty pounds overdrawn—will I please put this right at once ! "

She glared at her unoffending stepdaughter.

" It's absurd ! " she said. " Ridiculous ! Eighty pounds overdrawn ! Why, I never heard of such a thing in my life ! "

Eve smiled. She, at any rate, had had this experience before.

" I know what it is," said Mrs. Smith, with sudden decision. " They've got one of those wretched horse-racing bank clerks who is robbing the bank. He's filching my account because he knows I am so careless. I suspected it all along ! "

" The last time, mother," said Eve, quietly, " you thought Martha had been using your blank cheques. Why don't you fill up your counterfoils, and then you would know how much money you had ? "

Mrs. Smith offered no reply. She made a further rapid survey of the morning's post without finding satisfaction. She reserved two obviously private letters for the last. These she opened and read carefully. Then she folded them up, placed them in their envelopes, and slipped them into a bag which hung at her side, for all the world like a sabretache.

She scrutinised Eve with a long and approving glance.

" My dear," she said finally, " you've got to make a good marriage."

" Have I ? " asked the girl cooly. " I thought only people in novelettes made good marriages. What do you mean by making a good marriage, exactly ? "

"Now, don't be tiresome, Eve," said Mrs. Smith. "I've been a good mother to you. I've done my best to bring around you the most eligible men in London. I've spent money like water—which reminds me we shall have to have that kitchen range seen to—Martha tells me it's smoking again, and she can't get the oven hot—— Where was I? Oh, I was saying I have spent money like water, and I think I am entitled to some return. Not," she hastented to say, "that I expect any monetary reward for my sacrifices——"

Eve had heard all this before. In one form or another this conversation was almost a daily feature of her life.

"I can't help thinking, Eve," said Mrs. Smith, putting her head on one side and looking at her stepdaughter with her pale-blue eyes opened to their widest extent—" I cannot help thinking that you have not always appreciated my efforts. That new dress, for instance, which I bought at the summer sales : you have never worn it."

"It's totally unsuitable for me, mother," said Eve. "I thought I told you so. It is not the kind of dress that I should care to be seen walking in. I'd always much rather choose my own."

"That's pique," said her mother. "That's naughty pique."

Eve made no reply. It was useless to argue the point.

"Then the other night, when Mr. De Costa was here," Mrs. Smith went on, "you came down absolutely without a jewel on. Yet in your room, on your own table, for you to wear, are my own pearls, my own bangles."

Eve smiled kindly.

"My dear mother," she said, "I will not wear imitation pearls—not even to please you, and most certainly I will not wear any kind of jewel which everybody who is in the habit of coming to this house has seen round your neck at least a dozen times. You see, they are rather unmistakable," she said carefully. If they were real they could not be worth less than fifty thousand pounds."

"There is a certain finesse in these things," said Mrs. Smith, vaguely ; but she did not pursue the topic.

She waited until her own meal was nearly at an end, and the girl was folding her serviette preparatory to leaving the table, before she returned to the attack.

"What about young De Costa ? " she asked.

"What about him ? "

"Has he proposed to you ? "

"I really forget," said Eve, carelessly. "These people do

propose in a way, almost mechanically. Is that the dark little man with the blotchy face ? "

Mrs. Smith frowned.

" A most unkind description," she said severely. " His father is immensely rich. He would be a good *parti*. And Mr. Deane——" she continued.

Eve rose from the table.

" I do not propose to discuss these matters at breakfast, mother," she said. " You know it takes all the romance out of a thing. It reduces love and marriage to the level of cold bacon."

" But has he ? " persisted Mrs. Smith.

" Has he what ? " the girl evaded.

" Has he proposed to you, my dear ? Let me impress upon you the fact that Mr. Deane is enormously wealthy and enormously generous, and I hope you have not forgotten that he has been most kind to me. He has promised me——"

" He has proposed," interruped the girl, " if that is what you mean. In fact, he called this morning at five o'clock in order to make his proposal.

Mrs. Smith gasped.

I can well believe that. Martha Ann's description is more graphic and in the argot of her class. She said you could have " knocked Mrs. S. down with a feather."

An excellent opportunity for anyone who contemplated such an assault upon the little lady.

" Proposed this morning ! " she repeated incredulously. " At five o'clock ! "

" He knocked us up at five this morning," said the girl, " as Martha Ann will tell you, if you have any doubts."

" Why was I not aroused ? " asked Mrs. Smith, with a sense of grievance that she had missed something.

" Because he wasn't proposing to you," said the girl, calmly. " It was my affair entirely."

Mrs. Smith got up from the table, a little hurt.

" I think, Eve," she said, with a sort of stagey gentleness, that you might remember my anxieties and sacrifices."

" I do not forget them," said Eve, " only unfortunately, your sacrifices are not so much directed to my welfare as they are to your own affairs. That's a little unkind, isn't it ? " she went on. " But then I have said so before, mother. I do wish when we are alone you would drop this farce. Let us talk plainly to one another, and face obvious facts boldly."

Mrs. Smith sniffed and searched aimlessly for her handkerchief, but thought better of it. After all, Eve was not the sort of girl to be moved by tears. She did not need to have this fact again impressed upon her. Eve was hard. The dear Colonel, her father, had shown similar callousness, and had laid down the perfectly dreadful theory that the more one wept the less one perspired. And, indeed, he had written a paper on the subject, and had invited the Royal Society to allow him to read it—a request which was respectfully declined.

The subject of her marriage, as Eve had so truly said, had formed a periodic matter for argument, only unfortunately, in the present instance it was absolutely necessary that Mrs. Smith should know where she stood.

She had hinted as much, indeed she had said as much, before, but now she could say so in very truth. The eccentric behaviour of Long Island Gas was as nothing to the monstrous conduct of an oil well in Southern Russia.

Quite a lot of Mrs. Smith's money had gone from time to time towards the sinking of a borehole upon what the Directors invariably and carefully referred to as " The Property."

When they wrote to Mrs. Smith they referred to themselves as " Your Directors." It gave the good lady the comforting feeling that they were distant relations—though what satisfaction accrued to her from that, Heaven only knows.

" Your Directors," who had started out on their career joyful and optimistic, making conservative estimates of future profits, which were beyond the dreams of avarice, had grown rather gloomy of late. " Your Directors " had been probing the bowels of the earth without any great profit to themselves, and apparently without any great inconvenience to the earth. The oil, in its furtive, sneaking way, seemed to have got wind of " Your Directors' " intentions, and moved off to a neighbouring oil field.

" Your Directors "—sharp and cunning fellows—were not to be evaded. They purchased the neighbouring oil field, and told Mrs. Smith, by private letter, that the prospects were of the brightest and they soon hoped to make a definite statement.

After six months they made a definite statement—but the prospects were no longer of the brightest. The oil, in a panic, had retired some thirty versts.

" Your Directors " were considering their position. Mrs. Smith was impressed by the wholehearted devotion of " Your Directors " to her interests and the employment of that blessed word " versts " brightened her up. After all, it looked as if there were a mine somewhere, and undoubtedly it was in a foreign country where " miles " had a special name of their own, and so many other extraordinary things happened.

Her holding in the mine was comparatively small, but when she received the confidential letter which had been sent (though this she did not know) to some forty thousand other share-holders, she felt she would not be doing the dear directors justice if she did not use her knowledge to her own advantage.

So she instructed her broker to buy a large block of shares on margin, and in doing so she had her broker's enthusiastic approval. His name was Douglas Kenneth Gresham Macdougal. He was bald—spoke with a lisp—and in moments of agitation, fanned the air with his hands. The name inscribed on his insurance policy—and that, too, in which his property was made over to his wife—was Hendrik Solomon Eckstein.

He was something of an author : he had written and published a small book on " The Art of Investment." It bore the sub-title of " Making a Million—And How to Do It."

You might have thought he would have charged a fee for his tutelage—that the book itself would have been issued between covers of beaten gold at a sum within the reach of every millionaire.

But no ! He gave this wonderful work to any person who applied for it. You had only to write for his *magnum opus*, enclosing a two-cent stamp, and he mailed it to you by return.

If by chance you put aside his little work, and attempted to forget it, he wrote you touching letters, and generally managed to slip into the same envelope a folder or two about his gold-mining proposition, that copper pool, or this promising oil field.

He adopted what I believe is known as the " follow up " system, which is something very similar to the system adopted by the tramp who persistently dogs the footsteps of the man with the big cigar, in the hope that sooner or later he will drop in for something.

In one way or another, as a result of poetic folders and dis-interested advice from Mr. Macdougal and other outside brokers with names reminiscent of the Old Testament, Mrs. Smith had lost some eight hundred pounds ; not a considerable sum to most of the people who lived in Upper Mayfair Street, and not one to bother even a woman circumstanced as Mrs. Smith was—the morning after the loss.

We can most of us bear up under our losses the day they occur—it is about three months afterwards that the processes begin to arrive.

Eve knew nothing of her stepmother's folly, or she would have worried much more than Mrs. Smith. As a matter of fact, that amicable lady did not greatly distress herself. She was obsessed with the idea that she was a born financier. She adjusted things. She had learned the financier's trick—which is, not to borrow from Peter to pay Paul, but to borrow from Peter, pay one half of Paul's demands, and utilise the other half for playing margin on sure enough stock.

In this way the debt to both Peter and Paul may be discharged with a bit of luck, and anyway Paul has had something on account.

Mrs. Smith had made up her mind to have a day with her accounts. She went to her den with that object. Unconsciously, perhaps, she had expected her accounts to sort themselves out of the chaos which marked the condition of each drawer, and arrange themselves in orderly little heaps on her desk. She was mildly surprised and a little disappointed to find that they had to be distributed by herself.

So, like many another person more highly placed than she, she gave up all attempt to get to the bottom of her financial position, and gave herself over to the consideration of what she would do if she had a million pounds.

She spent a profitable and amusing morning in this pursuit, and shopped recklessly all the afternoon in the million-pounds' spirit

Eve was left very much to her own devices. She had few amusements, and she did not count correspondence amongst them. Yet she spent the greater part of the afternoon at her writing-desk. She told herself, not once, but a score of times, that any letter to Tatham was unnecessary ; that she had said all she could be expected to say, and that any reopening of the subject on her part must inevitably lead to further meetings and would most certainly encourage herself in a hope which, she told herself again, had no foundation in her feelings towards him

Yet she was impelled to write. I am no psychologist, and I do not attempt to explain the state of Eve Smith's mind There is an obvious explanation, but it must be as obvious to the reader as it is to me ; and it was that, like the mushy heroine of the mid-Victorian novel, Eve Smith must have felt that Tatham was not wholly indifferent to her.

It is not unnatural that she thought a great deal more about him to-day than she had ever thought before, that his face would intrude in her thoughts, that his tall, straight, spare figure would everlastingly hover in the background of her mind.

For the first time in her life she felt the want of somebody and something.

She had experienced the need for material things before ; she had wanted a new dress, she had wanted a change of air, she had wanted some variety to the eternal eggs and bacon for breakfast ; but now her want was a big want, and it was growing in importance every hour.

She wanted to see Tatham, just to talk to him. She felt he would put her troubled mind at rest. Exactly why her mind was troubled she did not care to discuss with herself. She had no wish to retain Tatham as a lover ; she instructed herself in this self-evident fact over and over again. She felt very "sensibly" towards him. He was so strong and helpful and comforting : she did not love him—it was absurd to imagine she did—so she admitted.

But just now she would have liked to have had him around, to be on terms of equality and good-fellowship with him, to talk over those plans which he was so ready to hint at in his mysterious way.

She had often cut short these attempts at confidence. Time and time again he had been on the verge of disclosing to her the great plans which he had merely outlined that morning. Time and time again she had turned the conversation in her embarrassment to a less personal subject.

She regretted her lost opportunities.

This much she confessed. She did not regret having rejected the larger share of his life.

She wanted to write and say this, but of course it was impossible. Any letter was impossible. She tore up the one on which she was engaged, only to draw, almost mechanically, another sheet from the writing-case, and begin all over again—

"MY DEAR MR. TATHAM,
    " I feel that——"

There was the difficulty. What did she feel, that she could express without his misunderstanding ?

The littered waste-paper basket testified eloquently to the diversity of her feelings.

She got up from the little Davenport and wandered aimlessly about the house. She was dissatisfied with herself. She might have gone out, and she wondered why she didn't. She loved the open air, and it was her hour for the park.

Again she made no attempt to explain to herself why she had changed her plans. The explanation may have been, and probably was, that she did not wish to be out if Tatham—that persistent man—again called.

She desired to be good friends with him. She felt that he was the kind of man who ought to have good friends.

Here was sufficient excuse for a letter. She started her eighth sheet—

"MY DEAR MR. TATHAM,
    " I feel that——"

But perhaps he would misunderstand her. He was a very

optimistic man. Again, would he think she was a coquette, desirous of power without responsibility ? Was it fair to him ? By attaching him to her train, was she spoiling his chance of finding the right woman ?

Here again she was in a quandary. She could not picture the woman suitable for a man of Tatham's qualities. She thought very hard ; she went over all the girls she knew, one by one, and for reasons satisfactory to herself she rejected them as unsuitable.

And in her rejection she may have been a little scornful.

Anyway, Tatham was not *that* sort of man (so she said). He was no light lover ; of this she was certain. He was the type of man to whom love could only come once in a lifetime, and if it were misplaced or the precious boon rejected by the woman of his choice, there would be no question of a substitute.

Here, at any rate, was a definite idea, a firm estimate of his character, not to be shaken or varied by doubt.

Eve Smith pictured him in the future a silent, lonely man, impervious to the wiles of women, adamantine against the attack of the little god, going about his daily life, cherishing one fragrant memory.

I do not know whether she thought in exactly these terms, but I do believe that Eve, drawing this heroic figure, experienced a glow of comfort from her workmanship.

So he could take no harm, but, on the contrary, secure strength from their friendship. She began her tenth letter :

" MY DEAR MR. TATHAM,
    " I fell that——"

Would he be satisfied ? Would the flame of hope burn up, and might not her encouragement adversely affect his plans ? He had told her every moment of time was precious to him.

She remembered this with a sense of guilt and tore the letter up.

Mrs. Smith's slender stock of stationery might easily have been exhausted, but at a moment when Eve had almost decided what form the letter should take, Martha Ann announced Mr. De Costa.

The girl hurriedly concealed the letter she had been writing, pushed the waste-paper basket under the little table with her toe, and turned resentfully to the smiling young man, who had come mincing into the room.

Now this is a fact, which not only Eve but Martha Ann will vouch for, that never before had young De Costa been received with such distinction. Hitherto he had been a visitor. It is true he had conveyed to her, to the best of his limited ability, a sense of his devotion. He had been regarded by her mother as a possible suitor ; but now he had crept out of the background, and was an individual. He was a being who desired that which Tatham desired, and there had come to her a resolution, based upon an insane conception of equity, that he was not to receive any advantage which she had, of her own will, denied to the man who loved her.

She was shocked to discover that, although her mental attitude was one of indifference tinctured with politness, he for his part had progressed to a stage of friendship which bordered upon intimacy.

He smiled and offered his well-manicured hand with an air which, if it was not proprietorial, savoured of prospective ownership.

" And how are you to-day ? " he said.

He handed his hat to the waiting Martha Ann, without looking at the woman : a fairly innocent action, but significant to the girl of his attitude of mind. He was quite at home. He had been calling almost every day.

He walked to the window, thrust his hands in his pockets, and looked out. He was indeed terribly at home. She would not have been surprised if he had sat down on one chair and elevated his feet to another.

" I wanted to see your mother," he said, turning to her.

She walked across the room and rang a bell.

" Yes," she said, " I am sure mother will be glad to see you."

Martha Ann answered the ring with some celerity. If she had not been in a position to do so, at all times, I should have been without a great deal of very valuable information.

" Mr. De Costa wishes to see Mrs. Smith," said Eve, sweetly. " Will you see if she is disengaged, and ask her if she will receive Mr. De Costa ? "

She dismissed the girl with a nod.

De Costa could not have been pleased ; he was undoubtedly surprised, and when Martha Ann returned he was scowling thoughtfully at the worn pattern of the carpet. Evidently he had not employed the interval profitably.

" But I want to see you also," he said, as he made, reluctantly, to follow the servant. " I've got something very important to tell you."

"Oh, that can wait, I am sure ! " said Eve. " I'm going out."

" But I must see you," he said vehemently. " It's a matter of considerable importance. My governor is coming here in half an hour. We think you could help us considerably and help your mother too."

He smiled mysteriously.

" My governor likes your mother awfully," he said, " and he can do her a real good turn." He was very earnest.

" Mother would love that," said Eve, with a little smile.

"Look here," said young De Costa.

He glanced at the waiting maid at the door and then at Eve, meaningly, but she wilfully declined to take the hint.

"If we can do what we think with this fellow Tatham, your mother will be a rich woman," he said, lowering his voice.

He stepped back to notice the effect of his words, and was satisfied, for into Eve's face had come a considerable interest.

"This fellow Tatham?" she repeated.

"Yes—yes!" He nodded his head. "It's a secret; you know who I mean. The tall man who comes here—he goes under the name of Deane, but his real name is Tatham. I can tell you things about him that would make your——"

He was going to say "hair stand on end," but thought better of it.

"That would startle you," he finished, in lame substitution. "He's an awful scoundrel. The governor may get a warrant for him. That is one of the things he wants to see you about."

He was breathless with importance. Eve looked across at the expressionless Martha Ann.

"Just wait a little while outside," she said.

Martha Ann went, making protesting noises under her breath.

"Now exactly what does it all mean?" asked Eve. "You may sit down there, Mr. De Costa."

De Costa was delighted with the effect of his bomb-shell.

"Oh, all sorts of things. I could tell you things about Tatham——" he began again.

"Oh, don't promise, just tell me," said Eve, impatiently. "What has he done? Committed a murder?"

He looked at her cunningly.

"I'm pretty sure you know a lot about it," he said. "The fellow is quite gone on you. I could tell you some things that would make you——"

He looked down helplessly for a simile.

"Well, please do tell me something," she said, with asperity. "I wish you would be more explicit."

"I can tell you this about him," said De Costa. ' He took a low advantage of some information which came to him through my governor, and committed an act of piracy on the high seas. We are perfectly sure that he's the man; in fact, he has admitted as much to the governor and to myself.

"But if we can get a third party to corroborate our statement, we have him, high and dry. And it's not only that," he went on eagerly, "Tatham has discovered an island—we don't know exactly where it is, but from what the governor has found out, he's pretty sure that there's gold there. Now——"

He leant over towards her, emphasizing his points by smiting, at irregular intervals, the palm of his hand with his stubby finger.

" There's gold on that island enough to make us all millionaires. Tatham has got it, and Tatham is under the impression the island is English ; but if it is the island we believe it to be, it is not English territory at all, but Portuguese ! "

There was a triumph in his last sentence.

" We only want to know for certain, and my governor will go straight off to Lisbon and get a concession from the Government to work the gold in that island. All that Tatham has done will be valueless. You'll be——"

The door opened at that moment, and Mrs. Smith sailed in.

" Mr. De Costa," she said, shaking her head reproachfully, " I have been waiting for you."

" I am so sorry, Mrs. Smith," said De Costa, " but I have just been telling Miss Eve——"

" Miss Smith," corrected Eve.

" Miss Smith," he said hastily, for he was in some terror of the tone she employed. " I've just been telling her about Tatham."

Mrs. Smith bowed her head and seated herself.

" It's very interesting, isn't it ? " she said. " It reminds me of those adventures which one read about when one was a girl."

" But how do you know he has discovered gold ? " asked Eve.

" Well, we were not certain," replied De Costa, " and we should have been in the dark had it not been for dear Mrs. Smith."

He exchanged a friendly smile with her.

" But Tatham very stupidly gave the game away——"

" The Island's Hope Gold Mining Corporation," murmured Mrs. Smith, complacently.

Eve turned on her, cheeks burning, eyes blazing with anger.

" Did you tell ? " she asked fiercely.

" Of course I told," said Mrs. Smith, calmly. " I always take dear Mr. De Costa's advice in transactions of this description. As a matter of fact," she said, " I wanted to know whether the shares were negotiable. Expenses have been very heavy, and I found it likely I should have to realize some of my securities. When I mentioned to dear Mr. De Costa the Island's Hope he gave me the shock of my life. No such mine exists !

" Of course," she added carefully, " I do not say that dear Mr. Deane is an impostor. It may be that the shares are not yet issued, that the Company is not registered, but still it does look funny."

" So you see," De Costa went on, " we've got a very easy thing. His bogus company——"

" Do not say that," said Eve, coldly. " Anybody who

realizes what a generous man Captain Tatham is would realize too that, although the company itself cannot be traced in England, it may very well exist in Tatham Island."

" Tatham Island ! " cried young De Costa. He jumped up. " Where is Tatham Island ? "

She was silent. She could have bitten her tongue for her stupidity.

" He has told you ! "

He pointed a stubby finger at her accusingly, and Eve realized the full measure of her error.

" I knew Eve would know," said Mrs. Smith, admiringly.

" He has told you his name, too," De Costa went on rapidly. " Of course—Captain Tatham—not Mr. Tatham—eh ? Of Tatham Island ! Now it's all plain sailing."

" What do you expect me to do ? " asked the girl, quietly.

A look of blank astonishment came into the young man's face.

" Well, with the information we've got and with what you can give us," he said, " we can get to work."

" And do you expect me to betray Captain Tatham's confidences ? "

De Costa was deceived by the honey in her voice.

" Well, it's hardly that," he smiled. " We don't want you to betray anybody's confidence, but here's a chap who has got possibly a huge fortune to which he is not entitled—who is a thief——"

" I don't think we need go any further," she said, with unmistakable scorn ; " it is sufficient that one member of the family should act as your agent ; to spy upon and betray a man whose shoe-strings you are not worthy to unlatch ! "

De Costa was struck dumb with astonishment and indignation. As for Mrs. Smith, she felt the occasion demanded more than ordinary demonstration of her disapproval. She rose slowly ; just as Queen Victoria would have risen in the face of an obstinate and a naughty Royal Highness.

" Eve," she said, " you have hurt me."

" So, between you," said Eve, taking no notice of her mother, " you thought you could persuade me to commit an act of the basest treachery, to betray secrets which had come to me under circumstances flattering to myself, as though I were the veriest eavesdropping servant."

(Did Martha Ann, with her ear glued to the keyhole, feel any twinge of conscience, or change colour ? I doubt it !)

" And you ask me, moreover, to betray, not ordinary secrets," the girl went on, her anger rising. Her hands clenched, the flush had died from her face, leaving her unusually pale. She was trembling in every limb. " You ask me to betray secrets which would ruin his life, which would undo all the work of years, which would nullify all the devotion and self-sacrifice, both of himself and his men. Don't you realize," she went on, her voice rising, " what hardships they have endured—how they have suffered—how they have, by their own endeavour, come into their little kingdom ? And you want to make me an instrument to sweep all that effort, all that endeavour out of existence ? And you dare——"—she stamped her foot—" think I would lend myself to such an infamous plan ? "

Little De Costa withered under her fiery glance.

" I thought——" he stammered.

" You thought ! " she said scornfully. " You little rat ! "

Her scorn aroused in him all the latent evil in his nature. His face went purple and the veins on his forehead were swollen.

" I can make you tell," he almost whimpered in his rage. " Your mother and I know what is best. We understand the world better than you—I came this afternoon to ask you to marry me—to share what may be millions. I love you," he cried. " I would die before I insulted you as that man Tatham has. If you knew what he did——"

" Oh, tell me," she said with indifference. " I am tired of your threats of mysterious information."

He was silent for a moment.

" I'll tell you," he said. " Three days ago Tatham secured a special licence ! "

" A marriage licence ? " said the girl, quickly.

Something inside her heart froze. It was as though the foundations of life were slipping from under her. He saw the droop of her eyelids, and her convulsive grip of the chair nearest her, and was satisfied with the effect of his words.

" He had the audacity to get a marriage licence," continued De Costa.

Eve Smith shot an anxious glance at him.

" Audacity ? " she said. " Who was the woman ? "

" It was made out in your name," said De Costa.

The colour came and went in the girl's face, her hands covered her eyes, momentarily.

" What do you say to that ? " asked De Costa.

Eve Smith said nothing, but her heart was singing a little pæan of joy, to a tune that was new and wild and wonderful, and altogether, so she told herself, unmaidenly.

XII

THE EVIDENCE OF THE FOURTH WITNESS :
RICHARD CALLUS (*continued*)

Dovetailing, as I have, and as I shall, the evidence of one witness with another, one fact is impressed upon my mind, that autocracy fails until it admits domination, that independence whether of character or state walks best when it leans upon another arm. There was much intelligence in Mad Peter of Russia : he showed this when he formed a mock court and played suitor to a sham Czar which he had set up above himself. Napoleon did best when he accepted advice, and the most powerful of European monarchs is the British King, who plays no open part in the government of his country. So it seemed that Tatham progressed farthest when he sought to fall into step with Eve Smith who walked at a slower pace, Mr. Callus impresses this truth upon my mind, and independent testimony consolidates this view. For Eve Smith was a strong and a pleasant character, worthy of Tatham's devotion, as the recorder shows.

TATHAM and I arrived in Doncaster the morning before the decision of the Portland Plate. He had rented a flat for us both, and he had, he told me, looked forward with keenest enjoyment to the prospect of spending four days at that delightful venue.

We spent our evening working out our scheme for the morrow ; our scheme was of course Tatham's, to which I offered from time to time my approval, or which was, at my suggestion, amended.

Tatham was in no great heart for the coming race. Something of the old enthusiasm, of the old dash, had died out. He seemed quieter, less inclined to oratory.

He was short of speech in those days, eminently practical, but his ideas were rather cold-welded, than hammered together, as they were of yore, in the white heat of enthusiasm.

Doncaster was very full, for during those years it was under royal patronage, and not only the King of England but a number of visiting royalties were being entertained at country houses in the neighbourhood.

Walking in the town that evening we had seen His Majesty driving through, and the sight of that popular monarch had re-established some of Tatham's enthusiasm.

During dinner I found him unconsciously reviving his old regal form of speech. It was " *We* would do this " and " *Our* Island." He even sketched a design for a new Tatham Island coinage upon the spotless tablecloth.

With the arrival of the trainer after dinner, we got down to the mundane business of racing.

Holton suggested that Tatham should defer his commission till the " draw " was known. As you know, a jockey going to the post draws lots for the position which he is to occupy at the start—a very important consideration, as, with a course like Doncaster's, the luck of the draw plays a big part in the result of the race. The best position is that on the rails. Two, three, four, five, and six are equally valuable.

The thing I feared about Tatham in his present mood, was whether he would be inclined to disregard such trifling matters, which, to the racing man, are vital ; I recognised his mood as a dangerous one, but he assured me the next morning, when we were taking our constitutional towards the course, that he had ordered almost all the machinery that was necessary, and there were only one or two accessories which were dependent upon the result of the day's race.

As to what the result would be, I took a gloomy view when the " draw " came to be made : for The Fighting Scout had drawn Number 17 on the outside right—sufficient to extinguish the chance, as I thought, of the best horse in training.

The trainer shook his head, and said he couldn't advise us to back the horse. But two people were absurdly sanguine of success ; the one being Tatham himself, and the other Plant, the jockey.

" If The Scout were drawn on the outside of the rails," he said, " he would jump 'em, lose a dozen lengths and still win."

I did not share the jockey's optimism. In the first place, we were meeting a number of very good horses, horses absolutely at the top of their class in this sort of event. In addition, there was the disadvantage of the terrible " elbow " where the horses on the extreme flank were crowded out, and found their characters dissipated for good.

Holton very sensibly took my view, and recommended a small investment, but Tatham had been looking forward to Doncaster, which is the heaviest betting race meeting of the year, and he had laid himself out to add substantially to his financial reserve without endangering his prospects.

I was in the ring when the market opened. It was a case of " 8 to 1 the field " at first, then there came a rush for one or two horses ; heavy commissions from one quarter or another brought the market to " 10 to 1 bar two." The Scout was steady at 100 to 6. I backed him myself, taking 500 to 30 from Thompson, and 300 to 18.

The ring was a pandemonium of sound, and I walked into the paddock and sat down. I could not see The Scout, but I caught a glimpse of a green jacket at the far end of the paddock, and was going towards it when a man came rapidly from the ring and buttonholed another.

" The Fighting Scout is favourite," I heard him say, and realized that Tatham had yielded to his impulses, and had backed the horse heavily. I leave it to the judgment of those acquainted with such transactions to estimate the amount Tatham must have invested to bring such a horse from 100 to 6 in such a strong market as that made for the Portland Handicap. I do not care to suggest the amount lest I should be scoffed at.

As I know a number of the Press men—and your Press man is worth knowing—I accepted an invitation to watch the race from the top of the Press stand.

I got up in time to see the white flag fall. It was a perfect start ; the field went off in a line, like a regiment of cavalry— but only for a couple of seconds was that line preserved, for there began manœuvring for position. As they came round the elbow into the straight, I saw the cerise cap of The Scout run wide and mentally marked him out of the race. Four horses bunched together on the rails fought out the finish. It was a magnificent struggle, head to head they raced on, with the wire only a dozen yards away, and then, suddenly, instead of four there were five !

It was The Scout who seemed to come from nowhere to contest the supremacy. In two strides he had his head in front —he had scored his fourth consecutive victory !

" This," said Tatham, when I met him after the race, " settles the power station."

It was characteristic of the man that his next thought was a purely trivial one, from the point of view of our great enterprise.

The King of England was leaving for London, and Tatham would have it that we should go down to give him a cheer as he drove off.

The popularity of King Edward with the racing crowd is proverbial, and to the heartiness of his send-off Tatham's stentorian voice materially contributed.

We were making our way back to the ring when Holton came up with a telegram.

" This has been waiting for you on the board in the paddock," he said.

Tatham took it and opened it.

" I expect it is an anticipatory congratulation," he said.

He looked at the wire and his face brightened. Without a word he handed the slip to me. It ran—

" Come back to London at once. I must see you. Most urgent.   Eve Smith."

" What are you going to do ? " I said.

" Come along ! " was his reply.

He waited for nothing more. We passed out of the Grand Stand at a run. There were line upon line of motor-cabs waiting, and Tatham hailed the first.

" The station," he said, " as fast as you can go."

I had time on the journey to look up the trains. There was not another for an hour and that was a fairly slow one.

" Are you sure ? " asked Tatham, anxiously.

He took the local time-table from my hand and scanned it.

" We'll have a special," he said.

But his face fell immediately.

" Have you any money ? " he asked.

I had neglected, as a matter of fact, to draw my winnings from the bookmakers. I knew, of course, the money would be sent on, but, as it happened, I was at that moment nearly penniless.

" I am exactly in the same position," said Tatham ; " still, we shall see."

He was not, of course, short of a pound or two, but railway companies do not run special trains on Promissory Notes.

We went sufficiently fast to fall in at the tail of the King's procession. He was alighting at the reserved space on one side of the station when we were dropped at the other.

I saw Tatham's eyes narrow, and a little smile twinkle for a moment at the corner of his mouth.

" Come along," he said.

He walked boldly over to where His Majesty was taking farewell of the bare-headed officials.

Nobody challenged him. A police inspector looked at him dubiously ; but Tatham favoured him with so charming and friendly a smile that before the officer could make up his mind we had passed the barrier and had fallen in behind the King's party on its way to the station.

The Royal Special was drawn up at a red-carpeted platform. A railway official saw us and stopped Tatham.

" This is the Royal Special, sir," he said, uncompromisingly.

" I know," said Tatham, with a very knowing smile indeed.

" I beg your pardon," said the man, and stepped back.

Tatham opened an empty " smoker," got in, and I followed, my heart beating a little quickly at my own temerity.

" All you have to do," said Tatham, in an undertone, " is to sit tight ; in the meantime busy yourself by putting your coat and hat upon the rack. So long as you are standing so that some enterprising detective cannot see your face you are all right."

And so it proved to be. We had a breathless four minutes

waiting (it seemed like four hours) and then slowly the train drew out, and in a few moments cleared the platform.

" Now," said Tatham, " whatever happens, they can't throw us out."

We had not been seated long before a man came hurriedly along the corridor, looking into the carriages.

He stopped when he saw Tatham and I. He was a big florid man, unmistakably Scotland Yard.

" Hullo, gentlemen ! " he said, " I think you are in the wrong train."

" I think we are," said Tatham. " Won't you sit down ? I should like to explain why."

He handed the telegram to the King's detective, who read it at a glance.

" Oh, you're Mr. Deane," he smiled. " Well, now you're here, you had better stay. I hope you had a good win."

He chattered a little about the race and then he turned to go. He hesitated with one foot in the corridor and paused a moment.

" By the way," he said, turning to Tatham, " I suppose you know that somebody made an application for a warrant for you ! "

" For me ? " said Tatham, genuinely shocked.

The detective nodded.

" Yes ; the charge was one of piracy and other kindred crimes. The affidavit, however, was not sufficiently convincing, so the warrant wasn't granted."

I wondered how this man, whose sole duty it was to guard the monarch, had become acquainted with the everyday gossip of Scotland Yard's inner circle. His next words explained.

" You see," he said, with the ghost of a smile, " we have been watching you for three days. We know something of you, Captain Tatham.

He shook his finger with mock severity.

" We were afraid you might attempt to usurp the throne of England ! "

I heard him chuckling as he went along the corridor. Tatham, however, might have said with Queen Victoria, " We are not amused."

" That is a monstrous suggestion," he snapped, and his voice expressed both pain and indignation.

.   .   .   .

It is a fact that the English police are very chary of accepting extraordinary charges. Senhor Don Alphonzo did not doubt for a moment that he had but to walk to Scotland Yard, frame his elaborate indictment of piracy, and secure at once the necessary *lettre de cachet* which would effectively remove Tatham from his sphere of activity.

Scotland Yard, having first treated him as though he were afflicted with a mild form of lunacy, had put him through a most pertinent cross-examination with the object of eliciting the facts on which he based his charge.

De Costa hoped that the warrant might be secured without fuss, and all the evidence necessary to a conviction obtained from Tatham subsequent to his arrest. But the police are very practical, hard-headed folk, and they pointed out in the first place that the act of piracy of which the excellent Brazilian complained, had never been reported either to the police of Great Britain or to the Bureaux of the other nations.

Moreover, Senhor De Costa was a foreigner. And foreigners have the habit of picturesque invention; this is an insular British view and is probably devoid of any foundation of fact.

Tatham they knew by repute, though no representation had ever been addressed to the British Government on behalf of the Congo Free State.

You cannot grant warrants on hearsay, and although Scotland Yard deemed it expedient to report the circumstance to the Congo Government in Brussels, it had at that time received neither instruction nor request from the Government, and there was all the possibility of an extradition tangle which Scotland Yard had no wish to unravel.

De Costa senior met his son by appointment at a little *café* in Wardour Street. It was a pleasant September afternoon, but the old man was not particularly interested in meteorological conditions. It suited him that the dingy, stuffy little restaurant should be empty, save for the fly-flicking waiters, though Xavier De Costa, his son, something of a dandy, and irritated by the petty inconveniences of life, could have wished that his parent had chosen a more savoury rendezvous.

It was a quarter after four in the afternoon that the taxi-cab, which conveyed the head of the house of De Costa, drove up to the door of the restaurant, and the old man alighted.

He paid the cabman his exact fare, to that individual's annoyance, and came hurriedly into the *café*.

" Oh, there you are ! " he said, as he caught sight of his son in the corner.

He bustled into the seat opposite, ordered a Cognac, and when the waiter had departed, handed a newspaper across the table.

The young man looked in the stop-press column. He passed the paper back without a word.

"His horse has won again," said his father; "the man has the luck of the devil."

They spoke in Spanish, though the younger man, as a rule, preferred the language of his adopted country.

"But his luck doesn't hold," his father went on; "he has gone too far."

His voice was triumphant, and his son looked across at him in some surprise.

"I thought," he said, "that Scotland Yard would not move."

"I don't care a snap of my fingers about Scotland Yard," said the old man, "it is the concession. Our man in Lisbon has just wired to me that the Government will grant the concession at once. But there is a difficulty."

He lowered his voice.

"In those seas, where I know Tatham's Island is situated, there are half a dozen small barren rocks of varying sizes, any one of which may be Tatham's.

"Now," he said, we must know which is the one, and for this reason. It is going to cost me a fortune to secure the concession, and I have no wish to ruin myself and enrich those pigs of Ministers in Lisbon for the sake of securing rights over rock where there is no gold. One or two of the islands are undoubtedly English. I think it is the Ile du Diable that Tatham has found, but I am not sure, and I would rather postpone cabling my agent until I am absolutely certain that I am not making a mistake."

"It is the Ile du Diable," growled the young man.

"Are you sure?"

"I'm not sure," he hesitated, "but I'm fairly sure."

"That won't do," said his father impatiently. "Can't you understand the position? This concession-hunting means money. It means money paid down to-morrow to the department which will grant me the exploitation of mineral rights, and if I am in error, and have chosen the wrong island, I shall have to open the whole transaction again, renew my concession for another place, and probably have to pay twice as much. We must make certain."

He thumped the deal table with his fist.

"And you've got to find out!"

"But how?"

The old man did not reply for a moment. He took a long silver cigarette-case from his pocket, selected a Havana cigarette with his brown-stained fingers. He lighted it deftly, and untwisting one loose end puffed a cloud of smoke above his son's head.

" You must find out," he said again ; " you've told me, and I know for myself, that this girl, Smith, can locate the island."

Xavier De Costa shook his head.

" I'm not so sure she can," he said ; " at any rate, she wouldn't if she could."

" Suppose I were to arrange for Tatham to be arrested on a bogus charge," said the old man, " and then suppose I produced this girl as a witness ? "

Xavier's expression was unmistakably antagonistic.

" I won't have her brought into court," he said explosively ; " besides, there may be no need whatever to charge Tatham. I will give you my idea."

For two solid hours they were talking together. The old man had seen Eve that morning, and so she was not unprepared when, a little before seven, the industrious Martha Ann announced visitors.

It was not the hour that visitors usually called unless they were invited to dinner, and, as Martha Ann can testify, the dinner that night was of significant frugality. Mrs. Smith dining alone (and it was tantamount to dining alone when she had no other companion at the table but her stepdaughter) was an exponent of the simple life.

Martha Ann ushered the two visitors into the drawing-room, then flew to find Mrs. Smith and to warn her that three chops and a pint of desiccated soup was very poor preparation for a dinner-party, if it were to include Mr. De Costa and his son.

Eve was dressing, but came down within a few minutes of their arrival. The two men rose and favoured her with a bow as she came in.

She looked towards the older man to explain the visit, though it needed little explanation.

" I have called for your answer, Miss Smith," said old De Costa.

His son looked at him. He did not know till that moment that his father had made an earlier call at Upper Mayfair Street, and he wondered what was the proposition that the old man had put, and how far it affected his own immediate prospects.

" I have no answer to give you now that I was not prepared to give you six hours ago," said the girl, quietly. " I could not, even if I knew, put you in possession of the information you require."

De Costa shrugged his shoulders.

" Why don't you tell my father, Miss Smith ? " pleaded the young man. " It means such a lot to us, and to you and to your mother. I am sure she would persuade you——"

"My mother could not persuade me to do anything I thought was dishonourable and unworthy," she said, with a note of hauteur.

"You know the consequence?" said the old man.

Eve Smith was very pale. Young Xavier noticed this for the first time. There were lines about her eyes as though she had been a long time without sleep. There was, too, a tightening of the lips, which betrayed mental distress.

"I know what you threaten," said the girl, steadily, "that you will have Captain Tatham arrested and that you will subpœna me, and force me to betray the locality."

"But, father," stammered the young man, looking appealingly at his parent.

Old De Costa turned on him with a snarl.

"You be quiet," he snapped, "this is my affair. Leave it to me."

"Yes," he said, turning to the girl, "that is my intention. You can save your friend a lot of trouble, and save me a great deal of inconvenience, by telling all you know."

"You said you wouldn't say that," protested young Xavier to the old man. "You promised you wouldn't."

"Will you be quiet?" said the other, fiercely.

Something in his father's eyes, some unsuspected fierceness, cowered him and froze the words on his lips.

"By hook or by crook, I am going to learn what Miss Smith has to tell," said old De Costa, savagely; "this man has done me a grievous wrong, and I intend repaying myself for all the inconvenience to which he has put me, and for all the money which I have lost as a result of his act of treachery."

Distressed as she was, Eve could not help feeling a twinge of pity for the youth. He looked at her appealingly, as though mutely asking her to dissociate him from the acts of his father.

"There is no court of law in England that would force me to say what I did not wish to say."

De Costa shrugged.

"Your refusal to answer will be accepted as an answer unfavourable to the prisoner. If you lie, the judges and the jury will know."

"Have no fear," she said haughtily; "I shall not say anything which is not true."

It was at this tense moment that Mrs. Smith came in. She boasted her ability to take in a situation at a glance. Now she thought fit to justify that boast.

"Ah," she said pleasantly, with a genial smile which com

prehended both father and son, " I see you have succeeded in persuading my obstinate daughter."

" I have not yet, madam," said De Costa, putting on his mask of courtesy with an agility born of practice. " I don't doubt we shall succeed eventually," he said with a smile. " I have had to take a very serious line with Miss Smith, and I know that you will support me in my action."

" You may be sure, Mr. De Costa," said the lady, fervently, " that whatever action you have taken has the approval of one who is not only a fond and doting mother, but is also sufficiently a woman of the world to realize the disinterestedness of your action."

It was a speech almost worthy of Tatham. She turned to Eve.

" Eve," she said, with proper sadness, " I have never yet exercised that authority which my position and my age, and the regard in which I was held by that hero who has long since carried his sword to heaven " (she dabbed her eyes automatically), " entitles me. Yet I feel," she said firmly, as she drew herself erect as a queen mother would draw herself erect, " that I must, in this present instance, insist upon your taking a certain line of conduct, a line of conduct which will be beneficial to us all, and which will be creditable and worthy of the name you bear. Mr. De Costa has honoured me with his confidence."

There was a little exchange of bows between the two.

" He has told me what steps he would take in certain eventualities. For the honour of the house ! " she laid her hand with dramatic effect on the girl's shoulder.

Eve heaved a deep sigh. She put up her hand and took that of her mother's. It was not so much to demonstrate her affection as to relieve an intolerably melodramatic situation.

" There is no profit in talking to me like that, mother," she said quietly. " You do not help me, or help Mr. De Costa. The honour of the house, you may be sure, is safely in my keeping," she said, with her little chin tilted upward proudly. " It is indeed more in my keeping than it is in yours."

" But think of the Court,· think of the newspapers," wailed Mrs. Smith, " think of the scandal ! "

" I have thought of all that," said Eve, with a little smile. " I do not relish the prospect any more than you. If Mr. De Costa does this disgraceful thing," she shrugged her shoulders, " what else can I do but endure ? Under any circumstances " —she faced the old man squarely—" I will not tell you what I know about Tatham Island."

The opposition he was encountering had fanned the fury of the old Brazilian to a white heat of rage. The veins in his forehead were swelling, his voice trembled when he addressed her.

" I will know ! " he said, " I will know where that island is ! If you don't tell me I'll find a way——"

He stopped suddenly and looked over the girl's shoulder at the doorway, his mouth wide open, his eyes staring ; for Tatham had brushed aside the agitated Martha Ann, and had stood there, unannounced, for quite a minute.

XIII

THE EVIDENCE OF THE FOURTH WITNESS : RICHARD CALLUS (*continued*)

This short section is based upon Eve Smith's own statements to Mr. Callus and upon the independent testimony of Martha Ann Huggins. I have, as the reader will observe, entirely ignored the somewhat sentimental and wholly inaccurate " society novel " which Mrs. Smith thought fit to issue at her own expense. " The Noble Adventurer ; or, True Love Vindicated," claims to be based upon the facts of Tatham's courtship, but the sugary little literary morsel is wholly valueless as a guide.

THE girl, following the direction of the old man's eyes, looked round. I saw her face go pink and white, I saw her hands clasp and unclasp about her crumpled handkerchief, and at that moment I knew what Tatham did not know, that which he would not have dared to guess.

He walked into the room with his shoulders bent a little forward, his eyes peering from left to right, a trick of his when he was facing a peril, the extent of which he did not know.

" I thought I heard my name mentioned," he said softly.

He did not directly address Eve Smith, nor did he look at her, as far as I was able to judge.

Whatever faults old man De Costa had, cowardice was not one of them.

" I mentioned your name," he said loudly, " and I am telling you now, Captain Tatham, what I have told this young lady ; that if you inform me where your island is situated I am prepared to take no further action, but otherwise, I shall apply for a warrant for your arrest."

It was of course the maddest kind of bluff to put on a man of Tatham's calibre.

" Indeed ! "

Tatham was monstrously polite. The girl's eyes were fixed on him. Her face was a little drawn with anxiety. He smiled at her, an encouraging and understanding smile.

" We are under the impression," he said regally, " that you have already applied for the warrant, but that the authorities have refused to supply you with the necessary instrument to remove Us. As for the situation of Tatham Island," he smiled again, " We are prepared, at this moment, to tell you exactly the latitude and longitude in which you can find it. It is——"

" Stop ! "

Eve Smith it was who spoke. In her agitation she grasped Tatham's arm and shook it.

" Do you know why they want to know ? " she asked vehemently. " If you don't, I will tell you ; they want to know, because they can take it away from you."

" Take it away from me ? "

Tatham laughed.

" I think not," he said with emphasis. " I think not ! "

There was an awkward pause. The two men made as if to go.

" You shall hear again from me, Captain Tatham," breathed De Costa. " Although I admit the warrant has not been granted, yet in a day or two the necessary authorities will be received from Lisbon."

Again I saw that look of fear in Eve Smith's face. It was almost pitiful to witness her distress.

" We shall be ready to answer any charge you may bring against us," said Tatham, " and we would remark that it is no part of our desire to shrink from the ordeal of a public trial. We have supreme faith in the justice of our cause, and we do not shrink from the judgment of our peers."

I saw Tatham at that moment visibly warm at the very prospect of a State trial, with himself as the central figure. He even went so far as to select the venue, because, from subsequent conversation I had with him, I gathered that he favoured Westminster Hall, the scene of the historic indictment of Charles I, as being worthy of so important an issue as *Rex* v. *Tatham*.

Neither De Costa nor his son was anxious to hear the conclusion of the speech. I gathered this because they had long left the room before Tatham reached his peroration, which he had so skilfully and adroitly adjusted as to render the presence of the two men unnecessary to its dramatic effect.

The girl listened with patience which was beyond praise, though her mind and her heart were in a ferment, and though every moment's delay was torture to her.

As for Mrs. Smith, that wonderful and adaptable woman, she became the sole audience, as far as Tatham was concerned. It was she who supplied the murmured applause, who agreed with the deductions he made and inferences he assumed, though I am positively satisfied that they were totally incomprehensible to her. She sat with the proud and happy smile of the well-tested friend who had seen her loyalty vindicated.

At last Tatham's address on State trials came to an end.

" I want to see you alone," said Eve.

There was hardly a break between his last words and her request, so quick she was to take advantage of the silence.

" I have to explain why I wired for you," she said.

I have an idea this latter was for my benefit.

Mrs. Smith took me down into her den. She found in me a somewhat absent-minded audience, yet, nevertheless, she succeeded in interesting me in her confidences.

She had always believed in Tatham ; she thought he was a splendid man. She felt that he was greatly maligned ; she had invariably supported him in season and out.

As for me, like the Irishman of fiction, I heard with one ear and thought with the other. I wondered what was going on upstairs, and how long it would be before I could learn.

There are moments which every journalist experiences, when he would sacrifice a great deal to play the part of the fly on the wall. I know that many people exist who would hastily condemn this attitude of mind as being entirely reprehensible, who would refer to the " prurient curiosity " of the modern journalist, and imagine that in " prurient curiosity " they had coined an original phrase. But the actions and thoughts of human beings are infinitely more to me than the viscera of the everyday bug is to the modern entomologist—and it is a study which involves less discomfort to the subject of research.

It was months before I heard from Eve Smith precisely what occurred.

When the door closed behind us Eve found herself without words. She did not exactly know what words she required—always a handicap to the most nimble witted of us ; doubly a handicap to Eve Smith, whose mind for the moment was stunned by the immense potentialities and dangers of her task.

" I wired to you," she said at last, " because I wanted to see you."

He nodded.

" These people weren't worrying you, were they ? " he asked, " because you need not——"

" I know," she said hastily, " I know ! But I'm afraid of what they will do ; that they will force me to go on to witness against you, but I will never tell," she said, " never, never ! "

Tatham was looking at her in perturbation. It was a new Eve Smith he saw ; such an one as he had never dreamt of.

She took his breath away ; he felt himself shaking from head to foot, and at that moment he cursed what he thought was a recurrence of malarial fever. But there was no malarial germ in Tatham's veins at that moment. There was something within her that spoke to him, some message which went out in vibrant waves and shook the very centre of life within him.

For the first time in his life Tatham was speechless. He could say nothing : his tongue refused its duty, and Eve Smith was in no better case. For her throat had gone dry and husky, it sounded queerly hoarse when she spoke, and she was short of breath though she had made no recent or unusual exertion.

"Captain Tatham," she managed, "I wanted to tell you something—that is why I sent for you. It is a very, very extraordinary thing I want to say. Suppose they arrest you ?"

He shook his head. Even that possibility did not lend him words.

"Suppose they arrest you," she went on, in her new, breathless way, with her eyes shining and moist, and her lips parted because of the very physical discomfort of breathing, "suppose they ask me to go to the witness stand to testify against you . . . there is a law in England, do you know it ? . . . that no——"

Again she stopped : the words were so difficult and so impossible.

"There is a law in England," she went on again, "that a wife cannot testify against her husband."

The last words were in a whisper.

For a moment their eyes met ; he held them for a breathing space.

They sent for us an hour later. Mrs. Smith had reached the point of reminiscence where she spoke openly of her overdraft. I had read the rosy pamphlet of Mr. Kenneth Douglas Gresham ; I had studied with more than ordinary amusement his carefully framed letters which demonstrated why his optimism had not been justified by results ; I had examined the half-yearly reports of I know not how many gas companies, oil syndicates, and other gold bricks of the speculative world, and I had nearly come to the end of my patience, when Martha Ann, all a-flutter, came to summon us to the drawing-room.

I went up, perfectly certain in my mind that Tatham had come into his own. It needed no more than a glance at those two people, standing like children in the centre of the tawdry drawing-room, to tell me that my surmise was accurate.

Tatham did not make a speech ; it was an excellent opportunity, but he failed to take advantage of the occasion.

Mrs. Smith wept and shook her head, kissed Eve, and nearly

kissed Tatham ; was in turns mournful, jubilant, reproachful, and roguish, and expressed her conditional approval in exactly the same terms, and with exactly the same feeling, that she would have employed had the prospective bridegroom been young De Costa.

"And when," I asked, with the bland air of a privileged friend, " is this happy event to take place ? "

" To-morrow," said Eve Smith.

Mrs. Smith sat hurriedly down on a chair. She did not faint : it was an evening of wasted opportunities.

.   .   .   .

They were married the next day at Trinity Church, Mayfair. The special licence, which all the time, unknown to me, had reposed in Tatham's pocket-book, had served its purpose admirably.

I was at the wedding breakfast, hastily organized and supplied by Whiteley's without regard to expense.

In the midst of the breakfast, indeed, in the middle of Tatham's speech, I received 'phoned instructions to catch the 2.20 Continental from Charing Cross and report myself in Belgrade for duty in connection with the Austrian crisis. I did not see Tatham or Eve again for a year. By the time I had reached Serbia they had taken their departure from England, and the chartered ship which carried them had in its hold a complete houseful of furniture, ordered by Tatham two months before—he was a remarkably confident man.

XIV

THE EVIDENCE OF THE FIFTH WITNESS :
SIR GEORGE CALLIPER

For the moment, I leave Mr. Callus and interpolate the evidence of Sir George Calliper. Herein we shall see, as in a glass darkly, the machinations of the admirable Don Alphonzo de Costa. Although I interviewed Sir George Calliper, K.C.M.G., a month before I ran Mr. Callus to earth, I have reserved his statement for this place. I think I have told you that my conversation with Sir George occurred in Scotland.

A tall willowy man with a stoop, an iron-grey moustache, and laughing blue eyes that surveyed the world through gold-mounted *pince-nez*, he was courteous to a degree. He furnished me with the Blue Book containing the correspondence between the nations, for which I was grateful, as it helped me when I came to assemble my notes.

" I AM a Permanent Under-Secretary of State for Foreign Affairs, a post I have held since October 11th, 1896. I knew Captain Tatham by name, but it was mainly in connection with representations made to my department by M. Hollings, Minister of the Interior to the Independent State of Congo, and concerning the loss of a Government steamer, that I knew of him ; also I know of Tatham Island, though only recently under that name. It has always been regarded as British territory, though its ownership has been a moot point amongst the nations.

" Great Britain's title to the island seems very clearly established by the Tsai-Lang Treaty, and also by the Treaty of Buenos Ayres, and whilst our rights have never been contested, they had never been pressed, owing to the inaccessibility of the isle and the difficulties of securing a landing.

" In March 1906, however, we received a communication from Dom Pedro da Silva suggesting a joint conference to settle one or two small but vexed problems of territorial status. The communiqué was concluded by a significant paragraph, which you can read for yourself :

" ' It is not the intention of my Government,' it read, ' to deal with any question, save those I have outlined to your Excellency. More particularly do I refer to the undisputed rights of Portugal to the Île de Desolation, secured to this country by the Treaty of Leipsic.'

" I immediately replied, going over the main ground of the letter, and dealing with his concluding paragraph as to which I said (you had better see the Appendix to Blue Book No. 5 for the full text)—

" ' His Majesty's Government, whilst appreciating your Excellency's desire to arrive at a settlement satisfactory to both nations, in the above matters, would direct your Excellency's attention to a slight error in the description of the Île de Desolation. His Majesty's Government can trace no record, either in the Treaty of Leipsic, or in the correspondence that preceded the making of that treaty, which deals with the disposal of that island. I am advised that the words of the treaty which you have probably in mind, and which run " the mainland and islands west of latitude 9. 5. 5. west," have no bearing upon the island in question, which was ceded to Great Britain by the Tsai-Lang Treaty of 1864.'

" Beyond a brief acknowledgment, I received no communication from the Portuguese Government. That is to say, no immediate communication. A week or so after this, the Government of the day fell, and Senhor Diaz constructed a cabinet.

It was after he had taken office that a despatch was received from the Portuguese Foreign Office, which dealt in the main with the question of the liquor traffic in Portuguese East Africa. Coming as it did after the previous communication, the end of the letter was peculiar. After dealing with the Government's attempts to suppress the sale of drink among the natives, the letter went on—

" ' My Government feels assured that it need not point out to your Excellency the difficulties experienced in a territory so vast as ours in East Africa. Fortunately, we shall not be confronted with such a task in our forthcoming colonization of the Ile de Gama, which, as your Excellency is aware, is a Portuguese possession in the Southern Atlantic, and commonly known as the Ile de Desolation. This island, which was occupied by Portugal in 1783, possesses natural physical barriers against an illicit traffic, and my Government are satisfied that your Excellency will watch with sympathy our attempts to deal with this insidious evil in this colony.'

" I immediately replied, expressing the Government's sympathy with every effort made by the Portuguese to suppress so pernicious a traffic, and concluded—

" ' His Majesty's Government would assure your Excellency of its friendly interest in the projected scheme of colonization, although it is at the moment at a loss to locate the exact position of the island to which you make reference. The only " Ile de Desolation " of which we have any knowledge, is the island that is situated in Lat. 20. 5. 5. west and Long. 37. 15. 4. south, which, as your Excellency knows, is a British possession secured to this country by the Treaty of Tsai-Lang, and undisputably held by this country.'

" I would refer you to the Blue Book for the exact text of these letters, and for the letters addressed at a later date by Senhor Pinto Sculo, the Minister of Health. It was addressed to us through Lisbon, and ignoring all previous communications, opened a new question.
" It will be seen that the despatch refers to the ravages of sleeping sickness in Equatorial Africa, more especially in Angola, and that it states *inter alia*—

" ' In view of the seeming impossibility of effectively segregating the cases, and providing that isolation from climatic and local conditions which are scientifically necessary for the successful combating of the scourge, my Government has decided, in the interests of humanity, to establish an experimental sanatorium in its South Atlantic posssession, *i.e.* the Ile de Gama (commonly called the Ile de Desolation). Your Excellency is aware that this island was discovered by the intrepid explorer De Gama, on the voyage to South Africa, and has ever since formed part of the Crown possessions of Portugal. My Government are satisfied that in their disinterested efforts to forward their scientific investigations into the causes and treatment of *trypanosomiasis* they will be supported by the cordial and whole-hearted sympathy of your Excellency's Government.'

" To this I replied, forwarding the report of the British Commission on Sleeping Sickness, together with all the available data on that subject—

" ' As evidence of the desire of His Majesty's Government,' I wrote, ' to assist your Excellency in your benevolent and disinterested labours for humanity, I have the honour to forward, under separate cover, the pamphlets detailed in the margin hereof. His Majesty's Government for the moment is without exact information as to the proposed site of the sanatorium to which your Excellency refers, but understands that it must of necessity be situated in the vicinity of Java or the Australasian or Polynesian possessions of your Excellency's Government. The only South Atlantic Isle of that name, of which His Majesty's Government has any knowledge, is the Ile de Desolation, situated in Lat. 20. 5. 5. west, and Long. 37. 15. 4. south, a British possession secured to Great Britain by the treaty of Tsai-Lang and by numerous other conventions, which I feel sure it is unnecessary to specify, since the claims of Great Britain are beyond dispute.'

" On receipt of this third communication, I called for information concerning the island, and for particulars of any exceptional circumstance that would justify this newly awakened interest in the place.

" For some time the efforts of my department, supported as they were by the unsparing investigations of Mr. Christopher Angel, of the Foreign Department, of Scotland Yard, were without result, but a month later I received a report from the latter gentleman, informing me that a party of settlers had established themselves on the island, that gold recovery on an extensive scale was in progress, and that large quantities of the metal were being exported regularly *via* Rio de Janeiro. The information was that the settlers were of British and American extraction.

" The figures available did not seem to be reliable, but such as we have been able to obtain show the following gold exports—

1903	..	..	..	..	.. 2,000 OZS.
1904	..	..	..	..	.. 16,000 OZS.
1905	..	..	..	..	.. 200,000 OZS.

" A native labourer who had been employed on the island and deserted from the islanders' one ship, stated that there were over seventy men and two white women on the island ; that there were beautiful buildings, and that the white men worshipped a strange god, who was shaped like a horse.

" On this information, scanty as it was, a conference was called, in conjunction with the officials of the Colonial Office, and it was decided that geological survey should be made of the island, and it was further decided that a Gold Law similar to that in existence in the Transvaal should be brought into operation. In the meantime, a letter was framed addressed to the leader of the island party, calling upon him to render a return showing the extent and location of his mines, the quantity of ores extracted, and the amount of fine gold exported.

" A proclamation was also issued calling upon him to suspend all further operations until the appointment of a mining commissioner, and the formal Government proclamation of the Ile de Desolation as a goldfield.

" This letter and proclamation were cabled to the High Commissioner for South Africa, with instructions that they should be sent by cruiser to the Island. At this time we had no knowledge of the fact that Portugal had invoked the assistance and sympathy of the Triple Alliance.

" H.M.S. *Fox* was accordingly despatched from Simon's Bay.

" The Captain's report will be found in Blue Book No. 5.

" According to his statement he made the island on the seventh day, and found a small steamer anchored inshore.

" He says that work was in active swing, and the smoke and steam from the engines were plainly discernible some distance from the land. He was struck by the presence of the sheerlegs, and the admirable hoistage system that existed.

" He saw no sign of any life except on the steamer, and this he boarded, and was met by the master, a man named Hackitt, who informed him that the leader would be pleased to speak with him. To his surprise, the officer found that there was telephonic communication between the ship and the shore, and was thus able to at once open negotiations with the man he sought. Tatham, for such, as he then learnt, was the man's name, was extremely polite, and wanted him to make the ascent of the cliff.

" Captain Mainward accepted and, with his first lieutenant, was hauled to the cliff head. He was met by Tatham and his wife, whom the officer described as a most charming lady, and the proclamation was exhibited and the Government's despatch delivered. Captain Mainward reported that he was astounded by the progress made by the islanders, and the exceptional and surprising evidence of their industry.

" Already a little township had sprung up, tree-shaded boulevards and electric standards, and the roar of the distant stamp-mills gave the impression that this was one of the world's industrial centres. The result of Captain Mainward's interview was a written communication handed to him the next day by Tatham for conveyance to the High Commissioner for South Africa, a statement embodied in the White Paper that was subsequently laid upon the table of the House of Parliament.

" Tatham's letter was virtually a manifesto addressed to the Home Government asseverating his title to conduct mining operations on Tatham Island, free from all restrictions or dominion, taxation or Government supervision.

" Much of this document seemed to be utterly irrelevant to the matter at issue, such as, for instance, his passionate denunciation of Downing Street, and its ' unintelligent interference.' This reply was transmitted by the High Commissioner to His Majesty's Government, and the Foreign Office was in course of constructing measures for the enforcement of its instructions when there came the famous despatch of the 19th of May. This was addressed by Germany, Portugal, Italy, and Austria jointly, and was of such serious importance that a Cabinet Council was called to consider it.

" It was handed to the Principal Secretary of State for Foreign Affairs by the German Ambassador, and was signed by Their Excellencies, the Ministers of Germany, Italy, Portugal, and Austria. The exact text is now public property, and was a peremptory demand for the withdrawal of the American settlers, pending the calling of a European conference to determine the status of the island.

" To this, a reply was forwarded, covering the ground over which the Government had already gone, and repeating that it was impossible for this country to agree to the proposed scope of such a conference, since our rights were beyond controversy and beyond discussion. It was pointed out that the fact that gold had been discovered on the island did not in any way influence the determination of the Government to preserve the *status quo* in its South Atlantic possessions.

" On the 23rd of May, in consequence of disquieting information confidentially conveyed to His Majesty's Government, a South Atlantic Flying Squadron was placed in commission, and the First and Second Army Corps were warned for mobilisation.

" On May 27th, at the instance of the President of the French Republic, an exchange of views occurred in Paris, with the result that a joint commission was suggested. The objects of the commission would be—

" 1. To examine the claims of Great Britain and Portugal.

" 2. To create a ' General Act ' embodying all resolutions arrived at.

" 3. To assess compensation to the present occupant of the island in the event of his removal.

" Great Britain gave a tentative agreement to the formation of this Committee, stipulating for a unanimous agreement on the part of the commissioners as a *sine qua non* to its acceptance of the recommendations. The suggestions that the committee should assemble on the spot, either on the island itself or on a warship to be agreed upon by the parties, were accepted.

" The removal of a conference round which would centre so much public interest, and as to the deliberations of which so much wild and unfounded rumour would circulate day by day, was welcome to His Majesty's Government. The period of quiet that would necessarily follow the disappearance of the Commission into the unreachable wastes of the South Atlantic, the squashing of dangerous public comment, and the fact that the newspaper correspondent could not arouse alarm by idle speculation, all these considerations weighed with us, in agreeing to the conference in mid-ocean.

" On July 21st the Allied Squadrons sailed. They consisted of :—

GREAT BRITAIN

H.M.S. *Sutlej*
H.M.S. *Bacchante*
H.M.S. *King Alfred*
H.M.S. *Essex*

FRANCE

Conde
Gloire

GERMANY

H.I.M.S. *Mecklenburg*
H.I.M.S. *Fürst Bismarck*
H.I.M.S. *Prinz Heinrich*

PORTUGAL

Vasco de Gama
Dom Carlos I

" I might add that, as a result of information which came to me and which was to the effect that Tatham was an American citizen, an invitation was extended to the Government of the United States to be represented, an invitation which was declined on the ground that the presence of an American ship might lead to complications.

" America was apparently the only country in the world which did not claim territorial interest in the Ile de Desolation.

" The composition of the remainder of the commission will be found in the Blue Book 5, together with the report of its proceedings. The sailing of these squadrons has invariably and very often improperly been described as a ' demonstration,' but such a contention is without foundation or reason. There was no intention on the part of His Majesty's Government to make any parade of force against Captain Tatham, no reason existed at that period for such a parade, and most certainly, had the Government any desire to move against him, it would not have sought the co-operation of the Powers.

" The results that followed the assembling of the fleet at Tatham Island were not anticipated by the Government, and they had neither the power to avert the subsequent developments, nor the ability to foresee them."

XV

FURTHER EVIDENCE BY THE FOURTH WITNESS :
RICHARD CALLUS

I return to pick up the broken thread of the war correspondent's story. Mr. Callus gave me a few sidelights on the European situation, and informed me that Europe was as near to Armageddon as it is ever likely to be.

He also states that Tatham never urged his American citizenship from purely patriotic motives. He had no desire to embarrass the land of his birth with his troubles.

BEFORE Tatham left England he wrote asking me to get into touch with the Congo Government, and ask them to fix a price for the *Pealo*, and to advertise the same in *The Times*.

He asked me further to look out for this advertisement, and forward the cutting or cuttings to him at the earliest opportunity. According to his arrangements the *Scoutina* (*Pealo*) would be at the Rio de Janeiro in the last week of April in the following year : and he begged me, if I could manage, to come to him then.

This invitation I was not able to accept, fortunately for me, for the *Scoutina*, as I afterwards learnt, did not arrive until six months after the time Tatham had fixed. She brought with her 14,000 ounces of gold, and a long despatch from Tatham. There was a great deal too much rhetoric and too little information for me, but I learnt that Tatham had imported three hundred black labourers, that the mills were working, that the city was in course of erection, that the coal supply was all that could be desired, and that Eve Smith was a source of constant thankfulness.

Last June, when the Tatham Island crisis was at its height, I received the following. It was addressed to me at New York—

" By wireless to Rio, per s.s. *Scoutina*. Meet *Scoutina* at Rio third of July. Most urgent and critical.—NED."

Three days after I had received this message I left for Rio, joined the *Scoutina* (now the *Plaza Reina*) and sailed for Tatham Island, to watch the culmination of his plans, to see Ned Tatham at his zenith, and to wonder at Eve Smith, of Upper Mayfair Street, but for the moment arbiter of the world's peace.

I arrived at Rio on the last day of June, and was on board the *Scoutina* by the third of July. Hackitt was in command, but it was a different Hackitt to the sad and melancholy man I had met that memorable day off Loanda. For one thing, he was resplendent in a new gold-lace uniform, he was jaunty and cheerful, and seemed, like everybody else who was brought into contact with Tatham, to have absorbed some of that wonderful man's assurance and self-confidence.

The *Scoutina*, too, was fitted more luxuriously than ever she had been in the course of her chequered career. Concerning her Hackitt informed me, with some pride, that Tatham had discharged his liability to the Congo Government in full, that he paid all the traders of Loanda, and that, harking back to the ship, she had been thoroughly overhauled and new engines fitted in her.

Hitherto my voyages in the *Scoutina* had been remarkable for the fair weather we carried, but on this trip we struck a bad patch, and for a week we rolled incessantly with heavy seas, and a stiff wind to vary the monotony. I was not particularly sorry to sail into the halcyon seas in which Tatham Island is situated, and all the happier when, like a thin layer of bluish cloud, the flat crest of Tatham Island came up over the horizon.

Nearer and nearer we drew, till I could distinguish, like two thin matchstalks perched perilously upon the edge of the cliff, the sheerlegs of Tatham's hauling gear.

Hackitt put up a signal—not the ragged old signal pennants of other days, but spick-and-span little flags, and as he did so there came a puff of white smoke from the hillside and a reverberating " bang ! "

For the first and last time in my life I was received with a salute of seven guns !

Tatham took some of the gilt off the gingerbread by explaining that the guns were only dynamite cartridges, his stock of ammunition being jealously conserved.

He was the same old Tatham, not a bit altered. Dressed a little more tidily than I had known him in the old days, with a cheek that showed signs of regular shaving.

" Come and see Eve Smith," he said ; " she is in the council house."

The council house was a stone building half-way down Roosevelt Heights, and here, too, on the flat shelf of the hill, Tatham had built his township.

" We've got a doctor, of course," he said, as he passed a white bungalow, all frosty with clematis, and labelled in large letters " hospital."

" I found him amongst my boys, and packed him off to England to furbish off his diploma. We haven't any patients just now," he added regretfully, " but perhaps—— Hullo, here's Eve ! "

She came towards us with outstretched hand.

She looked more lovely than ever in her wide-brimmed sombrero, and her business-like walking kit——

It was a delirious day.   I inspected the dairies, and the cattle ranch, and the sheep on the side of the Fallier Alps.   I gazed at the foundations of the church, and stood in an attitude of respectful ecstasy before the big dynamo at the power station. I went through the crushing mills and was deafened.   I descended No. 1 shaft and inspected the galleries.

(" A hundred million tons of ore in sight," said Tatham.) I did homage before the stable of The Fighting Scout, most wonderful of Portland Plate winners, and duly admired the sheet of beaten gold above his manger, on which was recorded his victories—even to the Windsor Selling Handicap.

I climbed the hill and saw the searchlight apparatus ; in fact, I spent one of the most delightful and tiring days I have ever spent in my life.   Tatham was for taking me to see the fortifications, but I protested.

Here Eve Smith supported me.

" You haven't asked to see mother," she said reproachfully.

I had forgotten the existence of Mrs. Smith.   When I thought of her at all—and one thinks of everybody and everything on a rolling ship—it was as one who, as the result of her son-in-law's affluence, had wedged her way nearer to the Mayfair end of the street.   I could picture her queening it with the best of her class, employing a faded secretary to disentangle her accounts, spending an ample allowance and finishing up her financial year " overdrawn."

" Your mother ? " I said in surprise.

" The Dowager," corrected Tatham, gravely.

I thought he was joking, for Eve Smith's lips twitched ever so little.   I saw every play of emotion on her face, for I could scarcely take my eyes from her.   She had developed in some extraordinary way.   She had always been a radiant and a beautiful creature, but now she had that touch of divinity which love alone can give to a woman.

Here at any rate, I thought, were two people absolutely and completely happy.   Thank God, I have never had to reconsider my judgment in that respect, for Tatham and Eve Smith were ideal.

But Tatham was perfectly grave when he spoke of the Dowager.   She held her position as one reflecting credit upon himself.

Eve's mother had, I discovered, become the Dowager Queen of the Island. She had accepted her title in the spirit in which it had been bestowed.

A little way down the hill, between Tatham's home and the little township, her " Palace " had been built, and here she lived, contented and cheerful. I went down to call upon her, accompanied by Tatham and Eve Smith, and she received me graciously.

It was a staggering experience meeting ex-Mrs. Smith thus. She " we'd " me and " our'd " me till I was dizzy. She took herself so seriously. She had quite settled down to the life, and would not, I think, have exchanged it for any other. She made tender inquiries concerning the dear queens and the dear kings with whom I am popularly supposed to be in hourly communication, and dismissed us all most graciously.

" Mother just loves this," laughed Eve Smith, as we climbed the hill to Tatham's house, " and it is so nice to have somebody like her to look up to : it makes one feel so safe, so respectable."

" She stands for the law and the established custom of the island," said Tatham, seriously. " She is an influence."

There was so much to say and so much to do, so much gossip to retail and hear, that the afternoon wore to evening so rapidly that one could almost watch the passage of the sun across the heavens. I noticed that Tatham had learnt company manners, for he insisted upon my talking about myself. There was little, however, for me to say. I told him the inner history of the bomb outrage in Madrid. I explained why the Grand Duke Bossaroff had left Russia hurriedly. I gave him all the racing news I had accummulated during my brief stay in England, and exhausted my shop.

I had now time to observe Eve Smith, and was rather surprised to find she upset my pet theory concerning her. I had expected to find her the managing director of the firm of Tatham and Company. I had anticipated a development of that domineering spirit which, as I suspected, was only latent, and only waiting for an opportunity to find expression.

But I was agreeably disappointed. I had expected a certain superiority of demeanour when it came to the discussion of the island. A sort of " oh-yes-but-things-have-altered-since-you were-here " attitude ; but, on the contrary, she placed me with her husband as one from whom no mystery of the island was hidden.

One piece of information that Tatham gave me was especially interesting to me. He had, he said, a couple of two-year-olds that " could move," and when things settled down he intended coming to England for a holiday, bringing with him his fliers. He had entered one of them in the Derby of 1908. He showed me a portrait of Plant, whom he described with characteristic extravagance as " the greatest horseman of the age."

It was not until nigh on midnight that we got to the serious business of our meeting. He then told me of the visit of the *Fox* and showed me the proclamation. He would have read me his reply word for word, but Eve, with rare tact, saved me.

Coming to the action of the Government, Tatham, who seldom swore, said he would have been damned before he surrendered the fruits of his labours, his enterprise, forethought, and general ability to any Government, or the minions of that Government. He was prepared to pay a reasonable sum yearly towards the revenue of the Empire ; he was willing, he said, to donate a battleship to Britain (providing, he specified, it was called the *Eve Tatham*), but he would brook no interference with his rights. He was prepared to take the matter into court, and to carry it to the House of Lords, conducting his own case (a prospect which almost compensated any disadvantage that might attend the necessity), but he would not submit tamely to the rule of the island being taken from his hands, and given over to irresponsible officials who would allow " this fair land of ours " to be overrun by the refuse of Europe and the Colonies.

At this time Tatham knew nothing whatever about the action of the Powers—a move that was occupying public attention, when I left America—and I was able to throw a new light, and not the most roseate, upon the future.

" What," said Tatham, pacing the length of his big common room, " what ! Germany, Portugal, Austria—— Submit to that—— What is England doing to allow such a thing ?—— Where are her ships, where is her ancient valour, her intolerance of interference ? "

In this strain he went on till the blessed Eve brought to the proceedings an icy stream of reason. Here was the new Eve— a development of the Eve of the Smiths' breakfast-table who could discuss such world-shaking, system-shattering matters as overdrafts.

" My dear," she interrupted him gently, " we have already complained of the Government interfering in our affairs ; it is inconsistent to blame them now for not interfering more than they have done. Let us first of all learn what has been done, and what the Powers intend doing."

So I gave them all the information I had, supplemented by

a cable published in the *Jornal do Brazil*, which brought my information up-to-date, and Eve Smith was very thoughtful.

" It is evident," she said when I had finished, " that the British Government does not expect this Commission to arrive at any decision, and they have only agreed to such a fantastic arrangement in order to allow this bellicose feeling to die a natural death. So far as the Commission is concerned, we have nothing to fear.

" It will be abortive, as all European conferences are—the only result that we have to fear is that the Powers unanimously agree to England's Sovereign rights, and I have an idea that there is a factor which they have not taken into consideration —one which is likely to reconstruct the whole situation.

" Mr. De Costa is more dangerous than we imagined," she added thoughtfully.

Next morning Tatham called his men together, and I was interested to see how they had shaken down into their various positions—I almost said humble positions—without in any way losing their council-rights or forfeiting their claim to partnership in Tatham's undertaking.

The shepherds and cattle minders were on a level footing with the mine manager and the doctor ; the stable man, whose business it was to take charge of the horses, gave his opinion as freely as did Eve Smith, the ganger, the electrician, the store-keeper, the caterer—they were " Tatham's Men." Sorted into spheres for which their special knowledge best fitted them, but equal partners with Tatham in the great enterprise.

Tatham told me that he had laid down the rule of social equality " on the basis of utmost accomplishment." I found out that he meant, roughly, that it was required of every man that he should perform the task for which he was best suited to the very best of his ability.

It did not matter to him, he said, that " knowledge " in one case implied a highly scientific training, and in another case a deftness in wielding a broom. So long as the sweeper could manipulate his utensil in a more competent fashion than the chemist, so long as the chemist could employ his test-tubes to greater advantage than the sweeper could have done, Tatham was satisfied.

Tatham addressed them, for him, briefly. He stated the position very clearly, and if he permitted himself to dilate at some length on the " conscienceless rapacity of decadent nations," it was, in the circumstances, excusable.

The meeting ended with the passing of a vote of confidence in Tatham and Eve Smith.

I need not say that that remarkable girl was present throughout the discussion.

Between that time and the arrival of the fleets, work proceeded as usual, and I had an opportunity of exploring the island. Tatham took me to see the armaments. " I have got a two-gun battery on Eve Heights," he said—and then explained that Wilhelmsberg had been so re-named. " I have a four-inch gun overlooking Alphonso Bay, and a two-gun battery at Nicholas Point." He had purchased the extra guns from the War Minister of a South American Republic.

On the afternoon of the seventeenth of August, the look-out man on Sydney Head telephoned that the fleet was in sight.

Immediately we mounted the hill to watch the arrival of the warships. They came over the horizon in double line, ahead, the *Gloire* and the *Conde* leading, canopied under a thick black cloud of smoke. From where we were one could hear the blare of bugles and see nimble-footed men running to their stations.

Apparently they had no intention of landing, for they gave no sign either by signal or otherwise, of their desire to make our acquaintance. Tatham had expected a formal call, and had specially prepared the " cage " for them with carpets, and had donned his smartest kit for their inspection.

It is difficult to estimate how much this little act of discourtesy on the part of the fleet cost Europe, or what might have resulted had the nations risen to the occasion and met Tatham amicably. Instead of this they made no sign, save to turn their searchlights on the island that night, and the next—an act which Tatham chose to regard as a great impertinence.

Through our glasses we were able to see the Commission at its work. It sat on the aft deck of the *Essex*, protected from the sun by an awning. There was a table at which sat five men, and other tables piled high with documents and maps and books.

There were half a dozen other little men—they seemed absurdly small from where we stood—who bobbed up and down incessantly.

There were officers and guards and secretaries, and a whole fleet of steam pinnaces carrying important-looking people with portfolios.

For six days the Commission sat before they sent for Tatham. Even in summoning him they were guilty of criminal tactlessness, for with their courier came the two men Tatham disliked most of all men in the world.

We were standing at the top of the cliff by the neat little

elevator, waiting for the cage to come up. Only Tatham, Eve, and myself were present, with the exception of the two men who had charge of the hauling gear. The cage came to a stop by the tiny landing-platform, and three men stepped out.

A Portuguese officer, an unshaven, swaggering, naval captain of diminutive stature, was the first to step out. He looked around with an insolent and appraising eye, and instinctively twirled his moustachios as he caught the gaze of Eve Smith.

But we hardly looked at him. The two men who followed were infinitely more interesting. The first was De Costa, the elder, in spotless white. By contrast his face was almost black.

His son followed, a little uncomfortably ; not the brilliant self-possessed youth we had known in England, but a haggard man, who seemed to have grown old all of a sudden.

I think he loved Eve Smith ; I believe he was almost big enough to make the supreme sacrifice for her sake. The will of his father dominated him ; he was but a pawn in the hands of the strenuous old man.

He stepped out from the cage reluctantly, as though he would much rather have been anywhere else in the world, and kept his eyes fixed on the ground, never once raising them to the woman he had lost.

I felt a little pang of pity for him, for I realized something of his feelings.

As for Eve, I do not doubt her sorrow was more poignant than mine, for she was a woman, and women feel these things.

" This is Tatham," said De Costa.

He grinned at the tall man maliciously, and his tone was as insolent as it could well be.

" Are you the man in charge ? " asked the officer.

He spoke English very badly, for which reason, probably, Tatham forgave him his offensive choice of words.

" I think, Captain Tatham, we may write ' Finished ' to your interesting biography," said the old man, venomously.

His hate had got the better of his discretion in that moment of triumph. " A half-breed, I think you called me ? "

He waved his hand towards the anchored fleet.

" There are enough breeds there to undo you, my friend. You shall have the experience of seeing your fine buildings in my hands. My island ! " he said exultantly. " Would you like to see the concession ? I can show it to you."

He fumbled in his pocket, though I am certain it was not there. As he spoke, the pent-up anger of years bubbled forth in an uncontrollable stream.

" You American thief ! " he hissed, and shook his fist with

great daring in Tatham's face. "I will have you turned from this island, bag and baggage! I will send you to a prison, do you hear?—you and your wife also!"

The Portuguese officer put out his hand. He said something quickly in the language with which I am not acquainted.

"You come at once to the Commission," said the officer, addressing Tatham. "As for my friend, you must not be offended, for you have done him a great injust."

"I'll go," said Tatham, between his teeth, "and your Commission will wish that they hadn't sent for me."

But there came a surprising interruption.

Eve Smith walked slowly forward.

"I will go," she said; "it is not necessary for my husband to appear."

The officer shrugged his shoulders.

"The Commission information desires," he said carelessly, "and little it matters whether your good friend comes or whether you yourself descend."

But Tatham was in a panic. He was, I think, seized with a notion that the Commission had sinister designs on Eve, that the whole thing was a plot to deliver him into the hands of the enemy.

"I will not allow it!" he stormed. "I will not trust these people!"

"You can trust me," said a sullen voice.

For the first time during the interview young De Costa raised his eyes from the ground and spoke.

Tatham looked at him long and earnestly.

"Yes, I'll trust you," he said quietly.

Young De Costa's face flushed. It seemed to make a man of him—that word of Tatham's. He squared his shoulders and lifted his head, and returned his father's scowl defiantly.

It was agreed that I should also accompany Eve Smith, this on the suggestion of young De Costa.

Before we left the island Tatham drew me aside and propounded all sorts of wild and improbable theories, concluding by slipping a revolver into my pocket with instruction to shoot the first man that laid his hands on Eve.

I pointed out that we would be on a British ship, and how absurd his fears were. I even went to the extent—Heaven forgive me—of talking sentimentally about the sacred protection of the Flag, and this last argument was convincing.

I shall not readily forget the expression of blank astonishment that came to the faces of the sedate Commissioners when the officer introduced Eve to the assembly.

Then ensued the following examination :—

The President : Do you speak French, madam ?

Eve Smith : Yes, monsieur.

The President : Can you speak it and understand it well enough to follow my questions ?

Eve Smith : Yes, monsieur.

The President : We have to ask you how long you have been domiciled on this island ?

Eve Smith : Three years.

The President : Are you related in any way to the head of the settlement ?

Eve : I am his wife.

The President : What do you, or your husband, regard this island as—I mean, what nationality ?

Eve : British.

The President : In settling here, were you induced in any way, directly or indirectly, by that belief ?

Eve : No, I do not think that the question of the island's nationality troubled us.

President : Did you receive any official sanction from, or notify your intentions to, the British Foreign Office ?

Eve : No.

President : If it were necessary—we are dealing with the matter hypothetically—but, imagining an occasion arose for the adjustment of compensation, suppose you were evicted, for instance, to whom would you look for compensation ?

Eve : To Great Britain, naturally.

President : For payment ?

Eve : Not necessarily, but for the support of our claim.

President : Because you regard the island as a British possession ?

Eve : No, because I regard myself as a British subject.

I could not help thinking that many of the questions addressed to Eve were fatuous in the extreme, but I did not know at the time of the suggestion that had been put forward at the conference, that Tatham was a secret agent of the British Government, and his occupation was part of a cunning plot to establish our title. There were a great many questions in the same vein, and eventually Eve was told that she might withdraw.

But she did not go. She asked if she might be allowed to address the conference, and, permission having been given, she started. In many ways her speech was a noteworthy effort. Her French was faultless, her delivery and style perfect ; never once did she hesitate for a word or an illustration.

She began by detailing the circumstances under which the

island had been occupied by Captain Tatham. She dealt with the idealism that had inspired his labours, and hinted, I thought a little unwisely, at the potentialities of the future.

"So far as the International aspect of our occupation is concerned," she said, "we are not greatly exercised. The purely academical discussion of this or that moral right is unimportant by the side of our actual achievements."

She went on to review the circumstances under which various colonies had passed into the possession of the European Powers. Some by conquest, some by purchase, some by the mere process of discovery and populating.

There were certain set rules, she added, certain definite precedents, upon which the powers might rely in dealing with Tatham Island.

"But "—she paused at the " mais "—" in this particular instance you are dealing with a country which is in every way unique. It has natural defences which are unassailable ; it has natural resources which are inestimable. Not only does it produce provision for the sustenance of its people, but it produces the all-conquering means of supplying its every deficiency —gold. Never was there such a land, so favoured by every natural condition, as Tatham Island. Bearing this in mind, I voice the opinion of the community when I say that to whatever decision this Commission may come, it is, and must be, essential that the solution adopted should coincide with the views of the people of Tatham Island."

When she finished nobody spoke : they were dumbfounded.

Truly Eve Smith had dropped a bombshell in the midst of this august gathering.

Sir Wilfred Fexley, the English member of the Commission, was the first to find his voice.

"My dear young lady," he said in English, "you cannot oppose Europe."

Eve Smith tilted her eyebrows.

"What is Europe ? " she said. " It is a patch of land, some seven thousand miles away. The reprobation of Europe will not affect us, the walls of Tatham Island will not crumble before the blast of the European horn."

"It is too ridiculous," said Sir Wilfred, crossly. " There are such things as navies——"

"There never was a ship built that could shell Tatham Island," said Eve, calmly. " You have no gun—and there never was a gun that could reach us."

Young De Costa was waiting at the gangway to see us off. He was not returning to the island with us ; a boat was waiting to carry him to the Portuguese man-o'-war. He held out his hand to Eve Smith diffidently, in doubt as to how she would receive the greeting. But she took and shook it warmly.

" Good-bye, Mr. De Costa," she said gently ; " I think you are not taking as great care of yourself as you ought."

He shook his head. His eyes were on the deck : he did not raise them to meet her pitying gaze.

" I am all right," he said roughly.

He dropped her hand, turned abruptly, and joined his father, who stood with the officers of the ship and the Secretaries of the Commission, in the background.

Returning to shore in the little motor launch that Tatham had bought in England, Eve said that she thought she had given the Commission something to think about.

Tatham came down in the cage to meet her, and displayed the first sign of emotion I have seen on his part. He took her into his arms (I was more embarrassed than touched) and acclaimed her the best woman in the world. There was another council meeting that night. It lasted exactly five minutes—at the end of that time it was a duly constituted parliament—the First Parliament of the Tatham Island Republic.

I do not remember having seen Tatham quite so serious as he was on that historic night, when he threw down the gauntlet to the world, and proclaimed his independence and the independence of the island.

No dissentient voice was raised when he produced the simple constitution of the new republic, drawn up on a sheet of ruled foolscap, and unmistakably written in Eve's neat hand. No voice interrupted him when he began soberly and with a voice that trembled a little in the intensity of his feelings—

" Be it enacted——"

until he concluded—

" . . . By command of the President of the Tatham Island Republic.

" EVE SMITH TATHAM,
" Secretary."

The whole of that night was spent in preparing copies for transmission to the representatives of the Powers. Eve, seated before her typewriter—the stenographic art was the newest of her accomplishments—was indefatigable. Her quick fingers danced over the keyboard, her soft laugh resounded through the night. Tatham made tea for us. I was not idle, for I was composing, at Tatham's suggestion, a National Anthem

Grotesque as it may sound, that was my task, and I rather flatter myself that the hymn, which began—

> " We rose a people of the sea,
>   And grappled with our destiny,"

had some really fine lines.

The next morning Hackitt was deputed to deliver our message.

He returned to the island, and acting under Tatham's orders, the *Scoutina*, securely anchored fore and aft, was abandoned, the cage hoisted to the top of the rock, and the sheerlegs lowered. We had drawn in the plank that connected us with the world.

" Now ! " said Tatham.

There was a flagstaff on Cape Roosevelt, and towards this Tatham pointed.

As he did so, a flag was broken at the masthead and fluttered out to the wind.

An emerald green flag, with forty silver stars, and bordered with cerise. It was the flag of the new republic.

I recognized it.

It was the sheet Tatham had bought to cover The Fighting Scout on high occasions, and which, at my earnest representations, he had reluctantly abandoned.

As to what happened after this on board the *Essex* I have no exact information. I have been informed since that the British representative was furiously urged to storm the island, and deliver Tatham into the hands of the Commission, a course he refused to adopt—and very wisely, since there was as much possibility of " storming " the sheer walls of the island as there was of storming the high roof of heaven. Furthermore, the British admiral refused to take any punitive measures at all, pointing out the fact that he had received no instruction to interfere with the islanders.

A council of war was called, and broke up again in confusion.

Then the Portuguese commandant must have lost his head ; and how far De Costa was responsible for the action we shall never know. He got up his anchor, and moving clear of the fleet, opened fire at the *Scoutina* lying in her moorings. The first shot fell short, the second carried away the funnel and navigation bridge, the third was never fired.

For suddenly from the cliff overhanging Kipling Cove sprang a mushroom-shaped jet of smoke, and like a clap of thunder the explosion of Tatham's four-inch gun.

The Portuguese boat lurched over to her side and went down by the stern.

I was standing on the bluff, and, as the ship went lazily over

I heard a gasp at my side. Eve, white as death, stood staring at the doomed vessel.

" Poor boy—poor boy," she said softly ; and I knew that one man aboard the warship would have gone to his death cheerfully had he known.

I heard the bugle call to quarters, and the shrill wail of the bos'n pipes.

I saw the British ships swing outward as their anchors came up, and white-clad figures about the guns. Then on the *Essex* a string of flags went up.

" Cease firing : the attack upon you was unauthorized."

Tatham replied—

" Have ceased firing."

A little later came another signal.

" Are you willing to meet the representatives of the Powers ? "

Tatham replied shortly—

" No."

The men stood to their guns all that day and night. Tatham inspected the river, and reported that ingress was impossible that way. As a precautionary measure, however, he stationed a guard at the cave, with instructions to blow up the entrance, even at the risk of flooding the country, if danger threatened.

But the fleet did not attack. There were further conferences and councils, and one morning, four days after the sinking of the Portuguese, the ships got up anchor and stood out to sea.

We saw nothing and heard nothing for three months. What was happening in Europe we did not know, and cared less. Work went on in the island. The thunder of the mills by night and day alone broke the silence of our peaceful land. On the third of November the look-out reported a warship in sight. She was a white cruiser, and through a telescope I could distinguish the white ensign flying at the peak.

" She's British," said Tatham, and later he identified her as the *Fox*.

She came within half a mile of the shore and signalled.

" Can Captain come ashore ? "

We signalled " Yes," and the cage was lowered.

Captain Mainward came off in his steam pinnace.

He shook hands with Tatham and myself, and was very gracious to Eve Smith.

" There has been a devil of a row about you people at home." he said, after he had complimented Tatham on the prosperous appearance of the city, " and I have a letter for you from the Foreign Office. I know its contents, and I want to talk it over with you. I don't suppose you want to remain cooped up here much longer ? "

Tatham did not. Some of his men, I know, wished to get away and find wives to share their new life, and Eve Smith was particularly keen on the introduction of womenfolk into the communal life.

" It comes to this," said Captain Mainward, " are you prepared, in spite of Republicanism, or rather in addition to it, to recognise the suzerain rights of Great Britain ? "

" You ask me that seriously ? " said Tatham.

" Yes," said the skipper.

" We are," said Tatham, at a nod from his wife.

" Very good," said the officer. " Are you prepared to make an annual contribution to the revenue of Great Britain ? "

" We are," said Tatham.

The officer, without a word, handed the letter to Tatham.

" I will await your answer on my ship," he said.

He would not accept our invitation to lunch.

In half an hour Parliament had assembled, and the letter was placed before it.

Generally speaking, it embodied all that the naval officer had said.

The rough draft of the reply was read to the Parliament and approved, and Hackitt was the messenger.

We saw our little launch sweep out in a semicircle to the ship's side, and the captain, surrounded by his officers, meet him. A few minutes later—

" Look ! " said Eve Smith.

A little ball flew to the masthead of the cruiser.

A second later—

" Bang ! " went a gun on the *Fox*, and the ball was broken. On the breeze flew a green flag with white stars.

" Bang ! " went a gun again.

And I knew, as the British cruiser saluted our flag, that the Tatham Island Republic was officially recognised.